**STEPHEN KING**

# STEPHEN KING

## ~ Stories from Five Decades of Storytelling ~

**Hans-Åke Lilja**

**BearManor Media**
**2024**

STEPHEN KING



Published in the United States of America by:

BearManor Media

1317 Edgewater Dr. #110
Orlando, FL 32804

bearmanormedia.com

Printed in the United States.

Typesetting and layout by PKJ Passion Global

ISBN–979-8-88771-573-5

# CONTENTS

# Introduction

Welcome to my second book about Stephen King. Perhaps you are reading this because you read my earlier book, *Stephen King: Not Just Horror* (BearManor Media, 2023), and hope to find more similar information. Or perhaps you picked this book up to learn something in general about Stephen King. It is, of course, also quite possible that you just had nothing better to do and simply thought, perhaps this might be worth a few minutes. Whatever the reason, I hope you will enjoy the time we spend together. Together we will visit a number of carefully chosen moments during the last fifty years of Stephen King's life and career. But before we start on the book itself, I would like to mention a few things.

I have not considered the possibility that some of my readers may perhaps not have read or viewed any of the books and dramatisations I discuss, and consequently there will be "spoilers." More of them in some chapters than in others. So consider yourself warned.

In the course of five decades, Stephen King has published no less than 88 books, which makes one and three quarters of a second book each year. I can't speak for any of my readers, but personally I am impressed. I will however not discuss all of these books here. That would take a considerably longer book and an enormous patience on the part of my readers. What I intend to do is to divide his time as a professional writer into its five decades, and then point to things from each decade I find interesting and worth taking a closer look at.

There is always some difficulty in fitting specific events into a time frame as narrow as ten years, so I ask your indulgence if some of the specifics discussed sometimes happen to sprawl outside of the decade under consideration. Also note that I have chosen to count the decades as stretching from, first, April 1974, and until April 2024. The reason is simple. Stephen King's first book publication, *Carrie*, was published in April of 1974, and it all began. Which is why I chose to start with that month. (And of course, in May 2024, Stephen King's 89th book will be published, a collection of short stories and novellas entitled *You Like It Darker*, to inaugurate his sixth decade in books.)

I just gave you a specific figure for the number of books published by Stephen King. But that number quite often varies, depending on who is giving it. Some are wily enough to say only that he has published more than sixty, which is of course true but falls short of the mark: King has to date published 66 novels, five of them written in collaboration with others. But that leaves out his collections of stories, his non-fiction books, and – which is where the controversy really starts – his graphic novels, those collections of shorter work which have been assembled from writings already published in book form, and book publications of both a screenplay and a musical libretto. As well as a few other titles difficult to classify. My own figure includes, of course, all of his novels, his initial collections of shorter work, his non-fiction, and those other books that contain essentially his own writings. You'll find my list at the back of this book. Don't worry if you happen to disagree with my count; I'm fine with that. Incidentally, to make up a reasonably correct chronology, wherever it has been available, I have viewed the day of first US publication as the official date when any book was published.

Now go on to the story of Stephen King's first half century in books. I hope you enjoy it.

Hans-Åke Lilja

# The First Decade

## 1974–1984
## Carrie Is Born

On April 4, 2024, exactly fifty years have passed since Doubleday published Stephen King's first novel, *Carrie*. While writing it, King and his wife Tabitha lived in a trailer in Hermon, Maine. They already had the first two of their children, Naomi and Joe. King worked as an English teacher at the Hampden Academy and wrote in his spare time; he had already published a number of short stories and in 1971 had begun selling to *Cavalier*, a monthly men's magazine paying better than *Startling Mystery Stories*, to which he had made his first commercial sale in 1967 and sold a second story in 1969.

Initially, Carrie was intended to be another story to be submitted to *Cavalier*. But after only three pages, King found himself dissatisfied with the story and threw the manuscript in the trash. Tabitha found the discarded pages, read them and convinced King to get back to his story. He capitulated and continued the story, though mainly to accommodate his wife. His first finished draft this time was 98 pages.

In December 1972, he decided to develop what had started as a novelette into a full novel, mostly because he had no other satisfying idea to work on. He based his main character, Carrie White, on two girls with whom he had been in school. One of them came from a poor family and had to wear the same clothes every day; the other was from a deeply religious family. By combining them, he created his fictional Carrie. To add wordage to his story, he decided to insert fictitious stories from various sources, including *Esquire* and *Reader's Digest* magazines, to give alternate version of the events in the story. And after selling the novel, he revised it further, this time with help from his Doubleday editor, Bill Thompson. In his original ending, for instance, King had demon horns start to grow on Carrie and let her destroy an airplane flying above her; Thompson talked him into deleting those scenes, which King himself admitted sounded like something out of the John Agar B-film *The Brain from Planet Arous*.

Initially, King was to receive an advance payment of $1,500 for his book, but Thompson managed to increase it to $2,500 and sent King this telegram – since the Kings were not able to afford a teleophone:

STEPHEN KING
BINGO. CARRIE OFFICIALLY A DOUBLEDAY BOOK. $2500 AGAINST ROYALTIES. CALL FOR GLORIOUS DETAILS. CONGRATULATIONS. LOVE THE FUTURE LIES AHEAD.
BILL THOMPSON

The hardcover edition of *Carrie* had a print run of 30,000 copies and was released on April 4, 1974. On May 3, a copy of the book arrived at the offices of New English Library, the British subsidiary of New American Library, which had begun as a reprint paperback house but expanded into publishing hardcovers as well as original work. The president of New English Library, Bob Tanner, read the novel himself overnight and wanted to publish it in the UK. He sent a copy to the parent company, and New American Library offered Doubleday $400,000 for the rights to a mass-market reprint edition. New English Library published *Carrie* already in May 1974, and New American Library brought it out in the US under its Signet Books imprint in April 1975.

Under his contract, Stephen King received half of the paperback money, and was suddenly free to write full time. The hardcover edition of *Carrie* had moderate sales, estimated at between 15,000 and 20,000 copies, and the first Signet paperback edition had a cover with only a girl's face and the text, "A novel of a girl possessed of a terrifying power"; neither the book's name nor that of the author was given. But the paperback sold more than a million copies in its first year, and no book has since been published without his name prominently displayed.

*Carrie* was the start of Stephen King's career. In the ten years from its first publication and Spring of 1984, he published a staggering fourteen further novels, two collections of shorter stories, and one non-fiction study of horror fiction. Among them were some of his most famous novels, like *Salem's Lot* (1975), *The Shining* (1977), *The Stand* (1978), *The Dead Zone* (1979), and *Pet Sematary* (1983); there were also four novels under his pen name Richard Bachman and the first book of his multi-volume epic "The Dark Tower."

# Richard Bachman: A Story

***Bachman, who was a very private person, grudgingly agreed to this.***

In late 1985, the reading and publishing world was shocked by the news that author Richard Bachman was dead. Preeminent among those mourning him were his widow, Claudia Inez Bachman, and his friend Stephen King.

Bachman's first novel was *Rage*, in 1977, and he quickly published a further three: *The Long Walk*, in 1979, *Roadwork*, in 1981, and *The Running Man*, in 1982. All were published by the New American Library imprint Signet, and all were original mass market pocketbooks. But since the sales of Bachman's novels gradually increased, his publisher decided to move his next book to hardcover format. Due to the different format, Bachman would have to reveal some information about himself for the book jacket, which was also expected to feature a photograph of the author. Bachman, who was a very private person, grudgingly agreed to this.

The photo of Bachman published on the book jacket was taken by his wife Claudia, and a short biography was provided. It told readers that Bachman was born in New York, served for four years in the Coast Guard and after that worked for a further ten years in the merchant marine. After leaving his life at sea he settled in New Hampshire where he owned a medium-sized dairy farm while writing at night, since he suffered from wakefulness. With his wife Claudia Inez, Bachman had a single child, a son who tragically died in an accident not wholly dissimilar to something in one of Stephen King's novels: at the age of six, the boy fell through the rotted cover over a well and drowned.

In 1982, his doctor during a routine examination discovered that Bachman had a brain tumor. It was located close to the brain stem, but a long and complicated operation managed to remove it. Sadly, however, Bachman soon fell ill again and at the end of 1985 he suddenly died from cancer of the pseudonym, a rare form of schizophrenia.

After Bachman died no further news of him appeared, until his widow nine years later unexpectedly got in touch with his earlier editor, Charles Verrill, to tell him that while emptying her house to move out she had found a carton full of manuscripts in the cellar. Most of them were more or less finished novels, and the one that seemed to be in almost final state was entitled *The Regulators*. Verrill's opinion was that the manuscript was very similar to Bachman's earlier novels, and after only some minor changes, and with the consent of Bachman's widow (now Claudia Eschelman), Dutton published the novel in September 1996. A month later the film made from Bachman's fifth novel, *Thinner*, was released by Paramount. In it, a careful watcher will notice Bachman's colleague and friend Stephen King playing a small part.

*The Regulators* was also released in a limited special edition, where each copy contained a check signed by Bachman before his passing. The checks were made out to various individuals, one of them for instance to a certain Jack Sawyer as payment for the idea for a novel, and you can hardly help wondering what Mr. Sawyer thought about never having received his money.

What would become Bachman's last novel, at least so far, was however not *The Regulators*, but *Blaze*. The news that a further virtually finished novel by Bachman existed was disclosed by his old friend Stephen King during a public appearance in London on November 8, 2006, during a tour King made to market his just published novel

*Lisey's Story*. King said that the manuscript for the new Bachman book was in his possession, but the only thing further he would say about it at the time was that it was a very early novel, written already in 1973. During a press conference the next day, an enthusiastic Swedish reader (who happened to be identical to the author of the book you are reading) asked if King might disclose the title of the new Bachman novel, and this was when King confirmed that he was talking about *Blaze*.

The novel was published in 2007, and apart from a film made from his earlier novel *The Running Man* (1987), it was the last so far heard from Bachman. But who knows, perhaps, possibly, further manuscripts hidden in some cellar may be discovered and published. Who knows? Given how private a person Richard Bachman was while alive, it is certainly far from impossible that he may have written more that, so far, nobody has seen.

## Richard Bachman: An Explanation

**”As I recall, he was a surly fellow.”**

The preceding subchapter deals with an author who never existed. Or who does exist, of course, but whose real name is Stephen King, while the name Richard Bachman is just as made up as everything else about Bachman.

Stephen King initially intended to use ”Gus Pillsbury” as a pen name; that name had belonged to his maternal grandfather. The manuscript for Bachman's first novel, *Rage*, had made the rounds of New American Library's editors under the title ”Getting It On,” and with ”Guy Pillsbury” given as author, but when it became known that King was in fact its author, he quickly withdrew the manuscript but resubmitted it under its new title. When the publisher later asked which name to put on the book, King on the spur of the moment gave them the name ”Richard Bachman.”

Many have wondered why King wrote novels under a pen name. This is his own version of it, as published on his home page:

“I did that because back in the early days of my career there was a feeling in the publishing business that one book a year was all the public would accept but I think that a number of writers have disproved that by now. I'm one of them and the guy who writes the *Along Came the Spider* books is another one who's written two or three books a year. Danielle Steel usually publishes two books a year. So, the public will accept more than one book from a writer in the course of a year. The thing is one book is all most writers want to produce or can produce in the course of a year and some of them only publish a book every two years. Ed McBain is another novelist who publishes multiple books in some years and his original name was Evan Hunter. That's the name he's always published under, and he adopted the pen name of Ed McBain for the same reason I adopted Richard Bachman and that was that it made it possible for me to do two books in one year. I just did them under different names and eventually the public got wise to this because you can change your name, but you can't really disguise your style. The name Richard Bachman actually came from when they called me and said we're ready to go to press with this novel, what name shall we put on it? And I hadn't really thought about that. Well, I had, but the original name — Gus Pillsbury — had gotten out on the grapevine and I really didn't like it that much anyway, so they said they needed it right away and there was a novel by Richard Stark on my desk so I used the name Richard and that's kind of funny because Richard Stark is in itself a pen name for Donald Westlake and what was playing on the record player was "You Ain't Seen Nothin' Yet" by Bachman Turner Overdrive, so I put the two of them together and came up with Richard Bachman."

King dedicated the first four Bachman novels to persons close to him, which can be seen as taking an unnecessary risk. Not unexpectedly there were repeated rumors about King being Bachman, and he was repeatedly asked about it. In a letter dated in May 1981, King wrote:

"The rumor has gotten around that I am Richard Bachman, but it's not true. I know him and I believe he lives in Connecticut – as I recall, he was a surly fellow."

In August 1982, King again declared that he was not Bachman, though this time he also hinted at knowing the name was a pen name:

"I'm not Richard Bachman, but I know who he is, and I can't tell. Professional ethics, and all that!"

*Thinner* was published in 1984, and two details in it are worth mentioning. One is that King at one point in the novel humorously refers to his own fame, writing, "You were starting to sound like a Stephen King novel for a while there..."

The other is the American edition of *Thinner* also, surprisingly, includes a couple of phrases in Swedish. What happened was that at one point in the novel, a curse is supposed to be expressed in Romani, a language which King is unfamiliar with. In a letter dated January 6, 1987, to his Swedish reader Lena Hansen, he tells us what happened:

> Dear Lena Hansen,
>
> I am sure this letter is coming to you long after you'd given up any hope of reply, but that is because I am a very sloppy correspondent. I was greatly amused by your letter, although it called on an old embarrassment to memory. When you say the words which are supposed to be in Romany are really in Swedish, you are right. When I needed a phrase, I simply picked one that sounded good from the Swedish copy of THE SHINING which happened to be lying on my desk. I then got in touch with a professional researcher, and asked if, for a price, he could find somebody to translate a number of English phrases into Romany. The phrases, of course were the ones you mentioned: White man from town, gypsy pie, and so on. In other words, the Swedish words were simply place-holders. I intended to take them out and replace them with the actual Romany. My researcher never replied. In the end, the book went out with all the crazy Swedish. But since

very few people read both languages, yours was only the second letter I've gotten on this subject although the book has sold over two million copies.

Best wishes,
Stephen King
P.S. I am including a copy of VARSEL from which the notorious? / famous words and phrases were drawn.

Due to this, we find phrases like, "Ta mig inte till mormor" (literally: "Don't bring me to grandma") and "Skummade igenom" ("Skimmed through") in the American version of *Thinner*. In the Swedish translation, they were replaced by nonsense words.

The *Thinner* hardcover jacket also carries a photo of Richard Bachman. But the man depicted is actually Richard Manuel, a friend of King's literary agent, Kirby McCauley. Manuel lived in Roseville, Minnesota, a suburb adjacent to St. Paul and Minneapolis, and worked with energy-efficient housing. He has later said that he told nobody, not even his sister, about his portrait being used in the book: "I didn't tell anybody, I was sworn to secrecy. Some friends called and said 'Hey, Dick, there's a guy that looks like you who's writing books in New Hampshire.' Even my sister called and said that."

McCauley said that he and King picked Manuel because "we had to find someone who lived a long way away from New York. There would have been a chance that someone in New York would recognize Richard Bachman walking down the street."

In spite of all caution, however, what should not have happened happened. Someone found evidence for King being Bachman. The man who did so was Stephen P. Brown, and in an article in *Wash-*

*ington Post*, April 9, 1985, two months after King himself had publicly admitted to being Bachman, he described what had happened:

"Novelist Richard Bachman died of exposure early this year.
I helped kill him.
My involvement began while I read Bachman's five novels. Gradually it dawned on me that they could have been written only by one man, and it wasn't Richard Bachman. It had to be Stephen King, the self-described "literary equivalent of a Big Mac and a side of fries" who had become one of America's most popular living writers.
My suspicions drove me to the Library of Congress for a look at Richard Bachman's copyrights. All but one was in the name of Kirby McCauley, who is King's agent. But the earliest of the Bachman books, "Rage," was in King's own name. I sent him a letter detailing what I had found and waited for a dissembling reply. Instead, one day, the phone rang.
'Steve Brown? This is Steve King. Okay, you know I'm Bachman, I know I'm Bachman, what are we going to do about it? Let's talk.'"

In the end, King chose to openly admit to being the author of the Bachman novels.

What could we have expected if Bachman's real identity had never been disclosed? King has stated that he hoped for his novel *Misery* (1987) to be the book that would take Bachman to the bestseller lists. In his postscript to *Nightmares & Dreamscapes* (1993), King writes that he had been working on two further Bachman novels. One of them was called *My Pretty Pony*, and was a gangster novel, but in the end King felt that he was unable to write the book he had envisioned and discarded all of it apart from a single flashback scene which was published under the *My Pretty Pony* title, initially as a limited edition of only 250 copies, illustrated by artist Barbara Kruger and published by the Whitney Museum of American Art in

New York City. It was later reprinted, both as a stand-alone book and as one of the stories in King's *Nightmares & Dreamscapes* collection.

The second Bachman novel King had worked on was called *Machine's Way* and was according to one rumor intended to be published by "George Stark," who was supposed to be a pen name for Richard Bachman. Parts of that book in the end turned up in King's novel *The Dark Half* (1989), which King initially wanted to publish as a collaboration between himself and Bachman. It wasn't, but King has said that he was inspired to write it by his Bachman experience, and it is dedicated to "The late Richard Bachman."

After Bachman's "death," two novels have been published under his name, *The Regulators* and *Blaze*. When the books were published, in respectively 1996 and 2007, far from all readers knew that Bachman was a King pen name; quite a few visitors to my Internet site asked me who Bachman was and what his relationship to King was.

In fact, both novels are the final versions of earlier King writings. *The Regulators* began as an original feature film manuscript, which director Sam Peckinpah read and wanted to make. But Peckinpah died in late December 1984, while King was working on a second draft of his manuscript. *Blaze*, in turn, was initially written already in 1973, years before *Carrie* had been published. But for its publication 34 years later, King rewrote and updated it extensively.

In 1985, an omnibus volume called *The Bachman Books* and containing the first four Bachman novels was also published by Stephen King's paperback publisher, New American Library. But on April 26, 1988, Jeffrey Lyne Cox held 60 students hostage at San Gabriel High School in San Gabriel, California, for over half an hour, though nobody was injured. A friend of Cox told reporters that Cox had been inspired by *Rage*, which he had read repeatedly and strongly identified with. Not much later, a copy of *Rage* was found among the possessions of Dustin L. Pierce, who on September 18, 1989, took a shotgun and two handguns to school and held a history class at Jackson County High School in McKee, Kentucky, hostage during a nine-hour standoff with the police. Again, nobody was injured, but due to his owning the novel, speculations that Pierce also had been influenced by the book began to circulate.

On September 11, 1991, Ryan R. Harris entered a mathematics class in Stevens High School in Rapid City, South Dakota, pulled out a sawed-off shotgun, ordered the teacher to leave and held the rest of the class hostage for four hours. Once again nobody was hurt, but Harris was also said to have been inspired by *Rage*. Then on January 18, 1993, Scott Pennington walked into an English class at East Carter High School in Grayson, Kentucky, armed with his father's revolver. He shot his teacher Deanna McDavid dead, then also killed school custodian Marvin Hicks and held the class hostage for twenty minutes. Shortly before the shooting he had written a book report on *Rage* and was upset when Ms McDavid had given it a C grade.

Finally, in December 1997, came the Heath High School shooting in West Paduch, Kentucky, where Michael Carneal shoots eight of his fellow students; three of them died. In his school locker, Carneal had a copy of *The Bachman Books* edition, including *Rage*. After this incident, Stephen King decided to let the book go out of print as an individual title, and to remove it from future printings of *The Bachman Books*. In a footnote to the introduction to *Blaze*, the seventh and so far, latest *Richard Bachman* novel to be published, King heaved a sigh of relief concerning *Rage*: "Now out of print, and a good thing."

The "Richard Bachman" name has appeared several times in other and less depressing connections. For instance, in an episode named "Caregiver," aired in season 3 of the series *Sons of Anarchy* on the cable network FX, Stephen King has a cameo part as a cleaner who helps others get rid of corpses. The cleaner's name is given as Bachman. And when *The Running Man* was filmed (premiered in 1987), King insisted that Bachman's name was the only one given to the author on whose book the film was based.

Will there be more from Bachman? I believe there will, and that he is far from gone forever. My bet is on him having hidden away at least one more book somewhere.

## A trip in the footsteps of King: Castle Rock, Maine

***Where author Thad Beaumont faked burying his pen name.***

Castle Rock, often called just The Rock by its inhabitants, is a small mill town in Castle County and known for its many strange and often tragic events. Since the 1920s, it is also the county seat, having taken that honor over from Lackery. Its closest neighboring town is Chester's Mill, but Portland is only 37 miles from The Rock, and South Paris is even closer, but Boston is almost 190 miles away. Though there is no record of its historical population, in 1959 Castle Rock had 1,280 inhabitants, and had by 1991 grown to around 1,500. But that year disaster struck when what locals call "The Big Fire" destroyed most of the town infrastructure and most inhabitants departed. During the last decades, however, the town has recuperated to at least some extent.

If you come as a tourist to Castle Rock, you should make sure to look at such places as the Juniper Hill mental hospital, the Homeland cemetery where author Thad Beaumont performed a faked burial of his pen name George Stark, the infamous Shawshank prison, the remnants of the once famous Suicide Stairs and The Mellow Tiger bar. If you have a morbid streak, you should also visit the Town Common Band Stand, where serial killer Frank Dodd murdered one of his victims in the 1970s.

We first heard about Castle Rock in the 1979 novel *The* Dead *Zone*. The town shares many features with Durham, where Stephen King grew up, and King found the name he gave it in William Golding's novel *Lord of the Flies*, where it is the name the shipwrecked boys give to "a narrow ledge of rock, a few yards wide, and perhaps fifteen long." It juts out into the Pacific, and on its left is an "impenetrable tangle of creepers and trees." Later, when the boys split into two warring tribes, Jack's group sets up its camp on the cliff, and name it Castle Rock. After introducing the town in *The Dead Zone*, Stephen King has returned to it in several novels and short stories. In 2018 and 2019, Hulu also aired two seasons of a horror TV show set in the town and its surroundings. The episodes were not based on any of King's stories, but most definitely inspired by his characters and themes.

You will find information on in which King novels Castle Rock appears at the end of this book, in indexes 2, 3 and 4.

# Unpublished books

***"and the pigs ate him."***

Are there really unpublished books by Stephen King? When does a man who regularly publishes at least one, and more often two new books every year find the time to write others which he decides not to publish? Reasonably, King himself is the only one who knows, but there can be no doubt as to his productivity, and he has many times mentioned books he has worked on but never published, but which he has put aside at various stages from just a few jotted-down ideas to partial or even completed manuscripts. Many of these works are deposited in the Stephen King Collection, which is part of the Raymond H. Fogler Library at Maine University. And some people have been there and read these unpublished works, among them the late Rocky Wood, who was an expert not only on King's published but also  his unpublished work.

The first of King's unpublished books is also unfinished, consists of only 76 manuscript pages and is called *The Aftermath*. King wrote it at the age of 15 in 1963, at the time of the Cuban missile crisis; it describes the world after a nuclear war has killed most of humanity. Eighteen- year-old Larry Talman is one of the survivors, and makes it his mission to destroy the evil Sun Corps, which now rules the remnants of the world. It is very doubtful if King will ever choose to finish this book.

King's next unpublished novel was completed in April 1970, and is called *Sword in the Darkness* (though the alternative title *Babylon Here* has also been used). It is the longest of King's unpublished books, at 485 manuscript pages or around 150,000 words, and was rejected by twelve publishers; King says that he considers it unpublishable and never wants it to be released. The main character, Arnie Kalowski, is forced to see his mother and sister die and later to take care of his father, who suffers from a nervous breakdown; later, he also experiences a race riot when a black activist lawyer speaks at a local high school.

In 1974, King started a book called *The House on Value Street.* It is a fictionalized take on the kidnapping of Patty Hearst by the Symbionelse Liberation Army, which she came to sympathize with and joined. But after several attempts, King gave up on the book; in his non-fiction book on horror fiction, *Danse Macabre*, 1981, he wrote: "It was going to be a roman á clef about the kidnapping of Patty Hearst, her brainwashing (or her sociopolitical awakening, depending on your point of view, I guess), her participation in the bank robbery, the shootout at the SLA hideout in Los Angeles – in my book, the hideout was on Value Street, natch – the fugitives run across the country, the whole ball of wax."

Two years later, in 1976, King started two novels, called respectively *Corner* and *Welcome to Clearwater.* Neither was finished, and although he has mentioned them, he has said nothing about their plots or about why he decided to discard them.

In 1977, King decided to write a novel set in England and centered on Dorothy Sayers' famous detective, Lord Peter Wimsey; the fragment is also titled *Wimsey.* All that exists is the first chapter of 14 pages and the first page of what should have been Chapter Two. These fifteen pages have been copied and are held by many Stephen King completists.

In the same year, 1977, King also started a novel called *The Cannibals.* However, he didn't finish it until 1982, during the filming of

George A. Romero's anthology movie *Creepshow*, written by King who also played the main character in one of the film's five separate stories. The complete manuscript to *The Cannibals* runs to 541 pages and is owned by King himself. The story centers on a number of people trapped in an apartment house, who in the end start eating each other. King later reworked the book and finally published it, now titled *Under the Dome* (2009). In 2009 King also made parts of his original manuscript for *The Cannibals* available to readers on his home page, and having read those excerpts I have to admit that I find it hard to believe that King "reworked" the book into *Under the Dome*. My guess would instead be that King used the basic idea for *The Cannibals* and wrote an entirely different book called *Under the Dome* but based on the same premises.

Some ideas intended to become novels have instead ended up as short stories, when King has become dissatisfied with how the novels progressed but found parts of his work still to his liking. His two short stories "Morning Deliveries (Milkman #1)" and "Big Wheels: A Tale of the Laundry Game (Milkman #2)," both in his collection *Skeleton Crew* (1985), are both parts of a novel called *Milkman*, which he began but never finished. "My Pretty Pony," in his collection *Nightmares & Dreamscapes*, is also an excerpt from a never completed novel, this time also supposed to be named *My Pretty Pony* and to be published as by Richard Bachman.

Another never published King novel is named *Doors*. Part of it was written in a notebook donated by King to a benefit auction arranged for the widow of Manly Wade Wellman (1903–1986), a fantasy and science fiction author and frequent contributor to the legendary horror fantasy magazine *Weird Tales*. Surprisingly enough, however, the notebook text seems never to have leaked; whoever bought it at the auction must be a very conscientious person.

In a 2000 documentary, King held up a book manuscript called *On the Island* and said that "It was about rich people who talked these street kids into going to an island and being hunted, with paintballs. And they get there, and they find these guys are actually shooting live rounds, and in my story, there were two or three who escaped and waited for the rich guys to come back." The book manuscript is 209 pages and is held by King, who, however, has stated that he doesn't intent to publish it. Possibly because the story might be considered to encourage violence.

At various times, Stephen King has also spoken of various story ideas without clarifying whether they have actually been developed in manuscripts or at just off-the-cuff notions. In an interview published in Douglas E. Winter's 1985 book *Faces of Fear: Encounters With the Creators of Modern Horror*, he goes into some detail about a story he suggested should be called "The Rats Are Loose on Flight 74": "I thought, what if somebody said, "I need a pillow," and the stewardess opened the overhead rack and all these rats came out onto her face and she started to scream, and the rats were biting off her nose and everything else, and one of the people in first class opened up a pouch to get an airsick bag because this was so gross, and rats came out of there, rats came out of everywhere. And the name of this story was going to be "The Rats Are Loose on Flight 74." I just haven't gotten around to writing it yet, but I probably will." And in an interview in late January 1988, he suggests another: "You know those kiddie rides in the malls? Well, what would happen if a mother put her kid inside a ride, dropped in a quarter and watched the thing spin a few times, and when it stopped, she discovered her son had disappeared?"

And there are many other similar quotes. In 1989, Stephen King spoke about trying to write a wild west novel, to be called *George D. X. McArdle*: "A few years ago, I did try very hard to write a western, because it's a form I like. I wrote about 160 pages and the only scene that really had any power was when the old guy got drunk outside the farmhouse and fell into the pigsty, and the pigs ate him. That one scene had some read drive and punch. This is what turned on my lights, for reasons I don't understand."

Or how about: "Husband and wife are at the airport to board a plane. The woman has to go to the ladies' room, so the man waits outside for her. And waits. She never comes out. Pretty soon he notices that other women are going in but not coming out. Boyfriends and husbands accumulate outside the bathroom, all feeling uneasy but reluctant to talk to each other. Eventually they alert airport security, then the governor and ultimately the president, in an effort to deal with the mystery."

Stephen King has also mentioned wanting to write a book on Jonestown and/or Jim Jones. In a 1989 interview he said, "I am interested in writing a book about what happened in Jonestown." A year later, he said, "What I would like to do next year – the idea has never left me – to write a book on Jonestown." So far, no such book has appeared. But perhaps someday…

Another book, which King himself claims is nothing more than a rumor, is *The Pretender*. When such a book began to be mentioned, in 1996, the claim was that it would be a "rock-and-roll novel." King's office later denied that King was working on such a book, and that its existence was just a rumor. What despite this indicates that the book may exist is on the one hand that reliable sources close to King claim that King has actually read from its manuscript in public, on the other an article in *USA Today* newspaper, which states, "King seems to be indicating the '60s and their lost ideals in *Pretender*, lambasting a 'generation of hypocrites'. He writes of a man telling his niece how 'we wanted to end war and racism but settled for a fax in every house and double-feature night at Blockbuster.' He sprinkles the novel with references to Jimi Hendrix to Michael Bolton to The Sex Pistols."

You may well ask why Stephen King would deny a book while actually working on it, but in fact he did the same while writing *11/22/63* (2011), admitting its existence only when it was announced for publication. Somebody close to King had mentioned that King was working on a book about the murder of John F. Kennedy, but King kept denying this ... until he stopped doing it. Perhaps something similar was true for this purported book, after which something made King give up on it and he went on to other projects.

What, if anything, will happen to these and other unfinished and/or unpublished books only Stephen King himself knows. Most probably they will just stay in his archives for the rest of his life. But on that hopefully far distant day when he no longer exists, someone may well feel tempted to market them. But that, too, of course remains to be seen.

# The Second Decade

## 1984–1994
## The It Years

In 1986, Stephen King published one of his most loved, read, and famous novels, *It*. The book introduced us to the Losers' Club and its members, Ben Hanscom, Eddie Kaspbrak, Bill Denbrough, Richie Tosier, Stanley Uris, Beverly Marsh, and Mike Hanlon. In the story we follow them as they revenge the murder of Bill's younger brother Georgie and in the end defeat Pennywise, the monster who most often appears in the guise of a clown, but who also is able to turn into whatever its victims fear most of all …

It took King over four years to write his book, but it is one of his longest: the first Viking Press edition runs to 1,138 pages. Initially his idea was to make Pennywise a troll, similar to the one in the Norwegian fairy tale *The Three Billy Goats Gruff*(first published in Norway in 1841, in English as translated by George Webbe Dasent in *Popular Tales from the Norse*, 1859). King's troll, however, would not be content with living under a bridge, but instead roam the entire sewage system under the town. Later, King asked himself what children are most afraid of, and decided on clowns. And even if a clown might not have been the most frightening creature anyone could have thought of before 1986, it had definitely become so now.

On his home page, this is how King himself describes the inception of *It*:

"In 1978 my family was living in Boulder, Colorado. One day on our way back from lunch at a pizza emporium, our brand-new AMC

Matador dropped its transmission - literally. The damn thing fell out on Pearl Street. True embarrassment is standing in the middle of a busy downtown street, grinning idiotically while people examine your marooned car and the large greasy black thing lying under it. Two days later the dealership called at about five in the afternoon. Everything was jake--I could pick up the car any time. The dealership was three miles away. I thought about calling a cab but decided that the walk would be good for me. The AMC dealership was in an industrial park set off by itself on a patch of otherwise deserted land a mile from the strip of fast-food joints and gas stations that mark the eastern edge of Boulder. A narrow unlit road led to this outpost. By the time I got to the road it was twilight--in the mountains the end of day comes in a hurry--and I was aware of how alone I was. About a quarter of a mile along this road was a wooden bridge, humped and oddly quaint, spanning a stream. I walked across it. I was wearing cowboy boots with rundown heels, and I was very aware of the sound they made on the boards; they sounded like a hollow clock. I thought of the fairy tale called "The Three Billy-Goats Gruff" and wondered what I would do if a troll called out from beneath me, "Who is trip-trapping upon my bridge?" All of a sudden, I wanted to write a novel about a real troll under a real bridge. I stopped, thinking of a line by Marianne Moore, something about "real toads in imaginary gardens," only it came out "real trolls in imaginary gardens." A good idea is like a yo-yo--it may go to the end of its string, but it doesn't die there; it only sleeps. Eventually it rolls back up into your palm. I forgot about the bridge and the troll in the business of picking up my car and signing the papers, but it came back to me off and on over the next two years. I decided that the bridge could be some sort of symbol--a point of passing. I started thinking of Bangor, where I had lived, with its strange canal bisecting the city, and decided that the bridge could be the city, if there was something under it. What's under a city? Tunnels. Sewers. Ah! What a good place for a troll! Trolls should live in sewers! A year passed. The yo-yo stayed down at the end of its string, sleeping, and then it came back up. I started to remember Stratford, Connecticut, where I had lived for a time as a kid. In Stratford there was a library where the adult section and the children's section was connected by a short corridor. I decided that the corridor was also a bridge, one across which every goat of a child must risk trip-trapping to become an adult. About six months later I thought of how such a story might be cast; how it might be possible to create a ricochet effect, interweaving the stories of children and the adults they become. Sometime in the summer of 1981 I realized that I had to write about the troll under the bridge or leave him—It—forever."

During the ten years from April 1984 through April 1994, Stephen King published 17 books and so reached a total of 35 books. Among the seventeen we find *The Talisman* (1984), a novel written in collaboration with Peter Straub, a new novel by Richard Bachman, an uncut version of *The Stand* (1990), and the second and third volumes of his epic "The Dark Tower."

## A trip in the footsteps of King: Derry, Maine

***Rumor had it that a man in a clown suit had been observed in connection with the murders.***

Derry is a small town in the state of Maine. It is close to Bangor, the third most populous city in the state as well as the county seat of Panobscot County, and some 120 miles from Castle Rock. Though Castle Rock is probably better known for its strange and tragic events, Derry has its own mysterious and at least as disastrous history. According to records, as early as 1741 some unknown disaster struck the fledgling Derry Township, and all of the original settlers, around 340, disappeared without a trace.

Gradually the town came to life again, and its history since the middle of the 19th century is fairly well recorded, not least the dramatic acts of violence which have marked it. In 1851, a certain John Markson fatally poisoned all of his family, then ended his own life by eating a poisonous mushroom. Then, in 1864, a gang of Confederate sympathisers, calling themselves the "Derry Padrinos," shot 120 of their town neighbors, fifty of them children. Only one child and ten adults survived. In 1879, the remains of a lumberjack crew of nine were found snowed in at their camp by the upper Kenduskeag river; all nine were dead and hacked to pieces. The Padrinos Gang notoriously killed five police officers in 1900, but two years later the gang members themselves were mysteriously killed. On Easter Sunday in 1906 a huge disaster struck, when one of the town's main industries, the Kitchener Ironworks, exploded. Eighty-eight children and fourteen adults were killed in the explosion, which occurred under the annual Easter Egg hunt. Finally, in 1935, the Bradley Gang were shot to death by vigilantes in the middle of town. Finally, and even earlier, a makeshift nightclub called "The Black Spot" had been founded by soldiers from a black unit of the Army regiment stationed not far from Derry. But in 1930, a group of racists from the Maine equivalent of the Ku Klux Klan, which called itself the Legion of White Decency, burned the clubhouse down since it made it easier for black soldiers to meet white townspeople. One of those surviving the fire was an army cook, Dick Halloran, who would later become head chef at the Overlook Hotel in the Rocky Mountain part of Colorado.

We first heard of Derry in a short story, "The Bird and the Album" (published in *A Fantasy Reader*, the program book for the 7th World Fantasy Convention, 1981) Later, the story was incorporated in the novel *It*. King has said that Derry is his fictional version of Bangor, though placed a bit west of the real Bangor. To a larger readership, the town became known when *It* was published, since most of the novel's action is placed there. You might wonder if this will increase or decrease the number of tourists.

If you are one of those still daring to take a trip to Derry, you should definitely visit the house at 29 Neibolt Street. By now it is in very bad repair and not a place anyone should really enter, but locals say that some strange creature lives in it, and so it is definitely worth taking a look at – from a safe distance. You should of course also view The Barrens, where the children in town like to play, and the Derry Civic Center, which has been rebuilt after the great flood in 1985. Those inclining towards the macabre should visit the remains of the Kitchener Ironworks, which exploded during the Easter holidays in 1906, killing over a hundred, most of them children. Many locals view the explosion as the end of the first of what was to become repeated periods of violence throughout the town's history, periods recurring more or less every 27th year.

Those visiting Derry might also find it of interest to visit The Standpipe, a huge water tower, the statue of Paul Bunyan in the park at the center of town, and of course the Derry Public Library. For more information on which novels and stories are set in Derry, see indexes 5, 6, and 7 at the end of the book.

## Working with a King: Peter Straub

***"Sold out? Christ, how stupid."***

The quote above is from Peter Straub. It comes from the interview that will make up this subchapter. The interview was published in July 2001, on both my own Internet site "Lilja's Library – The World of Stephen King" and on the Swedish site "Följeslagarna," which I co-run with Anders Jakobson, with whom I also interviewed Peter Straub.

Some background information concerning the subjects brought up in this interview may be helpful. For one thing, the film Mick Garris intended to make from *The Talisman*, and which is mentioned, never was made, and so far, neither *The Talisman* nor *Black House* (2001) has been filmed. Neither has the "bridge" intended to connect the two novels so far been written, though Peter Straub mentioned it several times when I spoke to him after this interview had been published.

*Black House* was published in the U.S. on September 15, four days after the 9/11 terrorist attack. The book went unnoticed among everything else that happened and never received the attention the authors had hoped for.

Peter Straub tragically died on September 4, 2022, from complications after having broken his hip, so King and Straub will never co-write a third novel about Jack Sawyer. Instead, Stephen King in August 2023, revealed that Straub before his death had sent him a long letter detailing his ideas about what might happen in a third book. That King publicly mentioned this makes at least me retain some hope that we may after all at some future date read that third book in the series.

**Lilja/Anders:** Can you tell us a bit about *Black House*? Word is that it's a darker book then *The Talisman.*

**Peter Straub:** By now, most people who care about it know the basic premise of *Black House*: that Jack is a retired detective who is drawn into involvement with a series of child murders. This case connects to the Territories, about which he now has amnesia.

**Lilja/Anders:** Maybe it's a stupid question, but did it feel like a natural thing to let Jack Sawyer age with the story? We mean - he was 12 in 1984 and now he's 31.

**Peter Straub:** It felt completely natural to catch up with Jack at the age of 31. In fact, I think it was easier for us than it was for him.

**Lilja/Anders:** According to King's official website there will be a lot of connections to his *The Dark Tower* series in *Black House.* This has been discussed quite a bit on the Internet. Some fans feel that you have sold out and that *Black House* is more Stephen King book then a King/Straub collaboration. How do you feel about this? Have you added any connections to your own stories to balance this connection to King's *Dark Tower*?

**Peter Straub:** Sold out? Christ, how stupid. Incorporating bits of the *Tower* mythology was my idea, and Steve of course agreed instantly. Partly, I wanted to find out more about that world, and I also knew that almost everything King writes these days is connected to the *Tower* universe. It's just a small element in *Black House.*

**Lilja/Anders:** In the interview you did for *Tenebres* Stephen King Issue last year, you said that *Black House* started with King remembering an idea you had mentioned during the writing of the first book. What was the idea?

**Peter Straub:** The idea was a reflection about just how bad a house could be, exactly.

**Lilja/Anders:** How did you (technically) write *Black House*? Was it different from the way you did it with *The Talisman*? We've heard about the 40 pages "bible", which sort of included the outline to the story - when did you write this "bible"? Was it only written by King?

**Peter Straub:** We cooked up the "bible" together over a week in Florida during February 2000. We talked about the story, then took turns sitting down at the computer and pushing the ideas forward.

**Lilja/Anders:** When you wrote *The Talisman* you imitated each other›s writing styles so you came up with a collaborative "voice" (King once said that you should have published the book under the name Chauncey Boogerheart, to stop readers from making a guessing game out of who wrote what in the book) - do you feel that this voice (Chauncey Boogerheart, if you want!) is present in *Black House* and in that case was it hard to find that voice again?

**Peter Straub:** This time around, Chauncey Boogerheart's voice is considerably more elevated, riper, plummier than heretofore. The direness of the situation seemed to call for an increase in dignity.

**Lilja/Anders:** When reading about how *The Talisman* came together (meetings in England and USA, long drives where you came up with the Territories, «the great Thanksgiving putsch» etc), it seems like you had a lot of fun writing the book. King once said,

"When Peter said he was going to send something, I would get excited because I was going to get to read some more of the story." As we've understood most of the work this time was done "electronically" - the long drives changed to daily emails for a couple of months, then a meeting in Florida (where the "bible" was written?) and the 50 pages installments back and forth as email attachments. Was it really as much fun this time as back in the early 80's when you wrote *The Talisman*? How many times did you meet and write together this time?

**Peter Straub:** Actually, this was more fun that the first time around. We got together only once, in Florida, and did the rest by email or in telephone conversations. Everything flew by, everything fell into place.

**Lilja/Anders:** Oddly, it seems like this method of writing was really effective since you finished the script six weeks before the deadline! Did this surprise you or is it a common thing?

**Peter Straub:** I have to say, it was a very happy surprise.

**Lilja/Anders:** From what we've read *The Talisman* should originally have been a «Go-get-it-and-bring-it-back»-book, but you decided to cut the outline in half since the book could have become way too long (you've said something about a 4000-page novel...) - what about this time? Did you write an outline that you knew would be enough for the length of the novel or did you have to cut it this time as well?

**Peter Straub:** Nope, this time we simply expanded on the outline. The first 2 pages of the outline took up about 50 pages of manuscript. The book wound up being longer than we had anticipated. It is almost exactly as long as *The Talisman*.

**Lilja/Anders:** Going back to the outline for *The Talisman* - do you remember anything from the part that was cut that you really wanted to write - a "kill your darlings" so to speak?

**Peter Straub:** I always liked the massacre in a farmhouse that was never written. It was inspired by the murders Capote wrote about in *In Cold Blood*.

**Lilja/Anders:** How do you feel about the fact that Mick Garris will turn *The Talisman* into a miniseries? Is this something you look forward to? Do you have any power over the script? One script written by Richard Lagravenese was very strange and not true to the book, but we know that Garris is writing his own script and that he will stay true to the book.

**Peter Straub:** Sounds pretty good to me.

**Lilja/Anders:** It's taken almost 20 years to turn *The Talisman* into a film (although the rights were sold before the book was published, according to the rumors, that is) - do you have any hopes for *Black House* turning into a movie? Seeing the «trailer» for the book (!) on the Internet gave us the impression that a movie was already made!

**Peter Straub:** The book has been sent to the various relevant parties, and we should have some information before long.

**Lilja/Anders:** We understand that there will be a special e-book version of *Black House*, one that will contain notes from you, King and the editor. Do you see this as a 20th century version of limited edition of the book?

**Peter Straub:** Well, there will be a limited, too, of course. I guess this added stuff is only an inducement, a sales tool, for the e-book.

Me, I don't know why anybody would want to read *Black House* in the e-book format.

**Lilja/Anders:** Early on there was some talk that King should write, what he called, a "bridge" between *The Talisman* and *Black House* on his own and publish this as an e-book. This book should update us on Jack Sawyer's life the last 20 years (roughly). This information came from King's agent Ralph Vincinanza in an interview in *Publishers Weekly*, but when we asked you about this, you didn't know anything about it. Do you know something about this now? Will there be a "bridge"? Are you involved at all?

**Peter Straub:** The "bridge" story is still completely up in the air. If it happens at all, I'll start it, and King will finish it. (If Steve reads this, he'll be surprised, because we haven't even discussed the matter. My editor thought I might begin it, then pass it along to Steve.)

**Lilja/Anders:** How do you feel about publishing on the Internet? We know King has published some stuff exclusively on the Internet (*Riding the Bullet* and *The Plant*); do you have any plans to publish on the Internet?

**Peter Straub:** I don't really write enough material to experiment with the Internet.

**Lilja/Anders:** *Black House* has already been promoted a lot - advertisements almost a year ahead of the release, websites, trailers, etc. Do you have any thoughts on this? Is this the future of promoting a new book?

**Peter Straub:** It may be the future of promoting a book considered highly marketable by its publishers.

**Lilja/Anders:** Will you and King do a signing tour for the book? If so, do you know any of the dates?

**Peter Straub:** No, there will not be a tour.

**Lilja/Anders:** Do you surf the Internet in purpose of seeing what your fans think of your work?

**Peter Straub:** Now and again, I use Google/Deja to find out if anyone's been talking about me.

**Lilja/Anders:** One of the readers once pointed out the similarities between King's *IT* and your *Floating Dragon* (how catastrophes with supernatural elements strike an American town in intervals and how it all ends with a struggle against a beast underground and how a group of selected people fight against the evil) - any idea how this happened since you wrote the books more or less at the same time?

**Peter Straub:** I seem to remember that we each read the other's manuscript when we were about halfway along, and probably that's how it happened.

**Lilja/Anders:** Do you think you and King will work together again? Can we look forward to *The Talisman* 3 in 15 years?

**Peter Straub:** I'd say the chances for a third volume look pretty good.

# The Golden Years of Stephen King

***Golden Years is a forgotten gemstone, deserving a closer look.***

On July 16, 1991, the first TV serial originated and written by Stephen King, and not based on any previous work of his, premiered on CBS. It was called *Golden Years*, and for seven episodes we could follow Harlan Williams (played by Keith Szarabajka) and his wife Gina (played by Frances Sternhagen). Harlan is 70, works as a cleaner at a top-secret government laboratory, and one night there is an accident – in fact, and more precise, there is an explosion caused by Doctor Richard X. Toddhunter (played by Bill Raymond), who is the story's arch-typical mad scientist. Two of Dr. Toddhunter's assistants are killed. Harlan, however, suffers only minor injuries, but is covered in a weird dust mixed with strange chemicals. What no one knows is that at the time of the explosion, Dr. Toddhunter was working on a top secret, non-sanctioned experiment aiming at rejuvenating dead tissue in animals, and in his eagerness, he ignored all precautions. Which sets it all in motion.

During an examination after the accident, nothing seems to be the matter with Harlan, apart from the strange fact that his eyelids glow green in darkness. The doctor expects this effect to shortly vanish. But Gina notices that Harlan's grey hair is beginning to regain its original color, and Harlan himself realises that his eyesight is improving. Harlan is in fact growing younger. Initially, both he and Gina find it hard to accept this but are gradually forced to do so. Government authorities, and particularly the secret agency called The Shop, and which readers will recognise from *Firestarter* (1980), begin being interested in Harlan. It covers up for Dr. Toddhunter in order for him to study Harlan further in order to recreate the specific mixture of chemicals created during the disaster. Harlan and his wife decide to escape and are pursued by The Shop agents.

The serial began with a double-length pilot (which is the reason for a rumor claiming that eight episodes of it exist) after which followed six weekly episodes, all initially aired Thursdays at 10PM. King himself wrote the scripts for the first five episodes; the two remaining were written by Josef Anderson. Initially, the plan for these first seven episodes to be continued by an open-ended series, but CBS decided not to renew the show after the initial season and the final episode was aired on August 22, 1991. King asked for a further four hours of running time in order to finish his story, but CBS would remain uninterested, and viewers were left to leave Harlan in the middle of his struggle both with his accidental rejuvenation and with the authorities.

When the series was later released on VHS and DVD, it was given a new ending, which, although far from conclusive, still gave watchers a more satisfying closure. The seven episodes had now been recut into a feature film, which was brutally shortened for its DVD and VHS version. Originally, the TV series had a running time of slightly over six hours; the DVD and VHS version was slightly under three hours. So, in fact, half the series was simply left on the cutting room floor. Anywhere from 15 to 30 minutes had been discarded in each 45-minute episode. If you search very diligently, you may find a Dutch DVD which actually does contain the entire series, except only the original series ending. That ending was shown only during the series' first run on American television in 1991, so the only chance of getting to see it is to find someone who recorded the last episode on VHS when it was first broadcast.

What, then, is the difference between the original and the later endings? The main difference is simply that the second version was made in order to give the serial a conclusion. In the original final episode, Gina dies from a heart attack while she and Harlan are trying to escape from The Shop. Harlan refuses to leave her and two Shop agents, Terry Spann (played by Felicia Huffman) and General Louis Crewes (Ed Lauter), who have left The Shop to help Harlan and Gina, are forced to abandon him. Harlan is captured by The Shop, and the episode ends with him lying tied to a cot while his eyelids burn green.

In the remade ending, Gina survives and escapes with Harlan. Jude Andrews (played by R.D. Call) from The Shop finds them, and to escape Harlan creates a green light into which they disappear. To some alternate world, to another time; who knows? Terry and Louis catch up with Jude and shoot him. And so, in the revised version, Harlan and Gina are – or so we at least can assume – finally free.

One interesting detail you may notice if you see both endings is that at least to me, it seems obvious that they were both filmed at the same time. Probably because those in charge of production had been told by CBS, had heard rumors, or guessed that the series might be cancelled. That the identical stage, which includes a burning house, should have been set up for a later reshooting of the final minutes, would reasonably have been too expensive for anyone to approve. So, we must conclude that those involved had the foresight to provide for a possible cancellation, and that kind of thoughtfulness is definitely not on common display.

*Golden Years* is an almost forgotten gemstone, deserving a closer look. The special effects are hardly up to today's standards, and some of the actors make little of their roles, but the serial is nevertheless an important piece of the Stephen King puzzle at least I am fascinated by solving. And among the pieces to be found in the show is a cameo appearance by King himself, who plays a bus driver, an obvious wink at Captain Trips in *The Stand* and one at Rainbird in *Firestarter*. The serial is definitely an interesting attempt by King to write an original TV series; he has said that it would have been impossible to do but for the success of David Lynch's *Twin Peaks*, which ran on the competing ABC network for a total of 22 episodes from April 8, 1990 to June 10, 1991. King said:

"Up until *Twin Peaks* came on, the only sort of continuing drama that TV understood was soap opera, *Dallas*, *Knots Landing*, that sort of thing. To some degree David Lynch gave them that. But he turned the whole idea of that continuing soap opera inside out like a sock. If you think of *Twin Peaks* as a man, it's a man in delirium, a man spouting stream-of-consciousness stuff. *Golden Years* is like *Twin Peaks* without the delirium."

# The Third Decade

### 1994–2004
### The green decade.

If Stephen King during his second decade tried his hand at an original TV serial, during his third he tested another first: a novel published as a serial. *The Green Mile* was published as an original mass market paperback serial, with one monthly volume from March through August 1966.

Why publish a novel in this fashion? The notion was suggested by King's foreign agent, Ralph Vicinanza, who said that he had learned from British publisher Malcolm Edwards, at the time at HarperCollins, that Charles Dickens often published his fiction in short instalments, either folded into his own magazine or separately as chapbooks which were sold door-to-door, and writing them while actually publishing them. King, who was having trouble getting into his next novel, felt that this method might be an interesting challenge – it would force him to both get on with his writing and to finish his book by a set date. While readers, on their part, would be unable to "cheat" by jumping directly to the end of the story and thus spoil its suspense.

When the novel was published in translation around the world, some publishers chose to issue it in a single volume, but many adhered to the way in which King had wanted the book to be published and issued their translations in six monthly instalments. Those who didn't may not have believed the six-part serial would succeed in their markets, or perhaps considered it too expensive. Personally, I enjoyed reading the book in parts. It was exciting to have to wait for a month between each new volume, never certain of what would happen in the next part.

The year after, in 1997, *The Green Mile* was published complete in one volume, and excepting a tenth anniversary limited edition, which was also in six volumes though sold together in a slipcase, this is how it has been reprinted since. It was also filmed, in 1999, directed by Frank Darabont and starring Michael Clarke Duncan and Tom Hanks. Along with *The Shawshank Redemption* from 1994, also directed by Darabont, it is one of the most highly rated of any of the films made from Stephen King stories.

During the ten years from 1994 to 2004, King published a further 18 books and reached the impressive total of 53. Apart from the already mentioned *The Green Mile*, he now published a book on his craft, *On Writing* (2000), a rewritten first volume as well as the fourth and fifth volumes of his "Dark Tower" series, and in 1996 the innovative novels *Desperation* (as by Stephen King) and *The Regulators* (as by Richard Bachman), set in two different imaginary worlds but with largely the same characters and thus mirroring each other.

## A travelogue: 39 hours in Bangor, Maine

***I also took the opportunity of putting my hand through the fence and pick up a small stone to bring back.***

In July of 1998 I spent 39 hours in Bangor, Maine. I went there with my then girlfriend, now wife. We arrived at ten to nine PM on July 26, landing at Bangor International, the same airport Laurel Entertainment used when filming its miniseries from King's story *The Langoliers* for the ABC Network, which aired May 14–15, 1995. Obviously, I expected to recognise the terminal; I had seen the miniseries and almost expected to stumble on one of those Pac-mans with sharp teeth I had watched on TV. But unfortunately, it was too dark to see most of the airport, so to me it looked just like any other airport I'd been to.

Almost immediately we were reminded of being in Stephen King territory. Already the cab driver taking us to our hotel told us that he often saw King walking around. We also drove by King's house, though the driver didn't tell us so until *after* we had passed it. But he did tell us that King had a favorite coffee shop where he often went to buy his coffee. If this were true, I have no idea. At any rate, we never found the place he had talked about, so it may as well have been a fabrication, told to impress us.

Next morning, July 27, the time at last had come to take a closer look at Bangor, county seat of Penobscot County and with a population of around 32,000 the third largest city in Maine. We started our tour at Betts Bookstore, at the time *the* bookstore for Stephen King enthusiasts (it still exists as a mail order business under the name Betts Books, but the store is sadly gone). While the shop was there, its owner, Stu, could get hold of any King book or story you were desperate to get. And I certainly wasn't disappointed: it was great to see the store in real life. In advance, I had emailed with Stu to warn him of our visit. He and his wife Penny turned out to be enormously nice and took the time to show us numerous rare books – collector's editions, ordinary first editions, signed editions and so on. After having spent over $110 in this unique bookstore (among other items for a copy of Richard Bachman's 1979 paperback *The Long Walk*), it was time to look at more books – this time in the Bangor Public Library, to which the King family has made huge donations.

Arriving at the library I obviously went to the Stephen King shelf. I had heard that the library supposedly held several copies of every book published by King, including the very rare *Six Stories* (published in 1997 as the sixth book from Stephen King's own publishing company, Philtrum Press, and printed in only 1,100 signed and numbered copies). But unfortunately, the tale of the library's treasure trove of King books had not only been a rumor, but sadly also a false one. What I nevertheless found was a copy of the first edition of Richard Bachman's *Thinner*, the last of his novels to be published without Stephen King's name appearing anywhere in the book. At the time I had never seen that edition, though nowadays a copy of it is also in my own bookcase. While there, I also took the opportunity to get a library card. Who knows, perhaps I might return some day. I still have my Bangor Public Library card, though I suspect it may no longer be valid.

Next on the agenda was at long last a visit to 47 West Broadway, the address to the King family home. Just as we arrived at the house, a car drove out through its gates. I saw that the driver was a woman, but I have no idea of who she was. We spent a few moments on the pavement outside the garden and saw three more cars leaving. The driver of one of them may have been Stephen King himself, but I saw him for only a few brief seconds and may well be wrong, though at the time I chose to believe that I had at least glimpsed King himself. In one of the two other cars was a woman, in the other an older couple. Again, I have no idea of their identities. A detail that surprised me was that the gates to the property were left wide open so that anyone could have walked up to the house and knocked. The claim that the citizens of Bangor genuinely respect King's privacy seems to be correct.

We spent a short while – well, all right, a fairly long while – outside the King residence. Apart from taking the obligatory photos, those showing me outside his gate and those focused on the bats guarding the gateposts, we also spoke to other enthusiasts on similar pilgrimages. Among them a group of Spaniards who seemed, if possible, even more exalted to be there than I myself. I also took the opportunity of putting my hand through the fence and pick up a small stone to bring back as a souvenir. I still have that stone.

After looking at the King house, we went on to look at the baseball field King has built behind his house (locals call it "Field of Screams," a humorous word play on the title of Phil Alden Robin-

son's film *Field of Dreams*, based on W.P. Kinsella's nostalgic baseball novel *Shoeless Joe*), and from there to the statue of Paul Bunyan, the same one that comes to life in *It*. Unfortunately, at the time of our visit the bus tour to all King-related places in town nowadays conducted by the same Stu who in 1998 owned Betts Bookstore didn't exist. Which meant we had to make our own way, which is far from easy in Bangor when you lack a car, as we did.

The next day we had to leave Bangor. On the way to the airport a new cab driver told us that he had been at college simultaneously with Stephen King, and that King already back then had been constantly writing. We spent only a short time in town, but it was still obvious that much revolved around King. Everyone knew of him, and many claimed some kind of connection to him, from having been to school with him to knowing his favorite shops. Once in the air I looked down on Bangor International Airport, and this time felt certain that I really did recognise if from *The Langoliers.* And didn't I see something a bit strange down there close to one of the buildings? Something that maybe, just maybe, reminded you of a Pacman, a Pacman with sharp teeth? Not that I can be certain, but…

## The Day the King Almost Abdicated

***"Ain't the two of us just had the shittiest luck?"***

On Saturday, June 19, 1999, at around four thirty in the afternoon, Stephen King was out on one of his daily walks along Route 5 in North Lovell, Maine, where his family has a summer house. On this particular day, King was in a bit of a hurry, since the kids were home on a visit and the family had decided to go to the movies. But he wanted his walk before it was time to go. Behind King, and going in the same direction, a man named Bryan Smith and living in Freyburg drew closer to King in his Dodge Caravan. As he later explained, Smith was on his way to buy "some of those Marzes-bars they have up at the store."

Shortly before Smith overtook King, he noticed that one of his two Rottweiler dogs, Pistol (the other one was named Bullet), was trying to get into the cooler he had in his car. While trying to keep Pistol away from the cooler, Smith lost control of the car just as he was about to pass Stephen King, and instead hit him. The collision was hard enough to break Smith's car window and throw King several yards. King was taken to Northern Cumberland Hospital, then flown by helicopter to Central Maine Medical Center in Lewiston. An eyewitness to the accident said that King "was breathing and laying in a heap and he was all tangled and I could tell his leg was broken."

Laird Covery, vice president of medical affairs for Central Maine hospital, said during the evening that King's condition was serious but stable, and that he was conscious and could communicate with his family. Later, the extent of King's injuries was also disclosed: a wide gash on his forehead, broken ribs, broken bones in his right hip and leg, and a punctured lung. Of his treatment, King later wrote, "those lower-leg injuries necessitated two deep incisions — they're called medial and lateral fasciotomies — to release the pressure caused by my exploded tibia and also to allow blood to flow back into my lower leg. If I hadn't had the fasciotomies (or if they had been delayed), it probably would have been necessary to amputate my leg. My right knee was split almost directly down the middle, and I suffered an acetabular fracture of the right hip — a serious derailment, in other words — and an open femoral intertrochanteric fracture in the same area. My spine was chipped in eight places. Four ribs were broken. My right collarbone held, but the flesh above it had been stripped raw. The laceration in my scalp took almost thirty stitches."

Numerous operations were needed to repair this damage, the first of them already on Sunday morning, June 20, in order to save his life. A second operation on Monday evening lasted for seven hours and fixed the fractures on his right hip and leg. A third on Wednesday lasted for ten hours and righted the injuries to his pelvis. The operation was successful and the surgeon, Dr. David G. Brown, said that only a millimeter differed between King's post-operation pelvis and his previously uninjured one. At a press conference after the operation, Dr. Brown was asked why the procedure had lasted for so long and he replied that King had been given the option of doing the entire repairs in a single operation or splitting it into two; King had preferred the single operation.

A fourth operation, to repair King's knee, adjust his pelvis and clean his wounds, was initially planned for June 25, but was postponed until the following week. Dr. Michael J. Serling, director of the Critical Care Unit at Central Maine Medical Center, gave the reasons for this: "Mr. King has undergone three major surgeries. He is tired and needs rest. In consultation with Dr. Brown and the King family, we've decided to postpone the next surgery until next week."

On Saturday afternoon, one week after the accident, Central Maine Medical Center posted an announcement on its Internet page. It stated that King after some rest felt much better. "His mood is improved; he makes jokes and eats full meals. He is like a new man." The hospital expected him to be fully recovered in from nine to twelve months' time.

On July 9, three weeks after the accident, Stephen King was released from Central Maine Medical Center, and the following day he posted an open letter on his home page:

"I want to thank everyone for their concern from the bottom of my heart. I have never been so shaken and touched and moved than by the concern that so many people have expressed for me. I am quite badly hurt, bedridden, but with all my senses intact. My doctors tell me that I should be able to walk again after a long period of recovery, and I hope you will keep me in your thoughts and prayers."

King had a further operation on August 4, this one to remove the pins used to stabilise his knee, and when he woke up following the procedure found that he was once again able to bend his knee. He also stated: "And in the midst of all this, something else happened. On 24 July, five weeks after Bryan Smith hit me with his Dodge van, I began to write again."

At the time of the accident, and for some time after, much of what actually happened remained unclear, but in his book *On Writing*, King in detail recounts the event. He describes meeting a car shortly before the accident. The two women in that car later talk about having passed Smith and seen his car sway from side to side on the road. One of them had said to her friend, "That was Stephen King walking back there. I sure hope that guy in the wan doesn't hit him." In the split second before being hit by the car, King had thought, "My God, I'm going to be hit by a school bus." The next thing he remembered was lying on the ground. He lost consciousness, and describes waking up again in this way:

"I am very carefully wiping palmfuls of blood out of my eyes with my left hand. When my eyes are reasonably clear, I look around and see a man sitting on a nearby rock. He has a cane drawn across his lap. This is Bryan Smith, 42 years of age, the man who hit me with his van."

Smith afterwards told friends that his first thought was that he had hit a small deer, but then saw King's bloody eyeglasses lying on his dashboard. When Smith saw that King was conscious, he told him that help was on its way. King remembered Smith as calm, almost cheerful. "Ain't the two of us just had the shittiest luck?" Smith said. King had looked down at his body. It seemed as if all below his waist had been twisted halfway round to the right. He looked at Smith, saying, "Please tell me it's just dislocated." To which Smith nonchalantly had replied, "Nah, it's broken in five, I'd say, maybe six places."

When King next regained consciousness, ambulance medics had arrived and King asked Paul Fillebrown, who was helping him, if he could have a cigarette. He couldn't. King asked Filleborn if he was going to die, and again got a negative reply. Two months later he phoned Filleborn to thank him. At that point he had realised that Fillebrown probably had saved his life by doing everything right from the first moment on. King also realised how close it had been when Filleborn said, "I've been doing this for 20 years, and when I saw the way you were lying in the ditch, plus the extent of the impact injuries, I didn't think you'd make it to the hospital. You're a lucky camper to still be with the program."

Later, King has stated:

“There’s a long gash in my scalp, the result of my collision with Bryan Smith’s windshield. This impact came at a point less than two inches from the steel, driver’s-side support post. Had I struck that, I likely would have been killed or rendered permanently comatose, a vegetable with legs. Had I struck the rocks jutting out of the ground beyond the shoulder of Route 5, I likely also would have been killed or permanently paralysed. I didn’t hit them; I was thrown over the van and 14ft in the air but landed just shy of the rocks.”

Dr. David Brown, when talking to King after the accident, confirmed that, ”You must have pivoted to the left just a little at the last second. If you hadn’t, we wouldn’t be having this conversation.”

There were several aftermaths to the accident. Smith was indicted on two counts, driving to endanger and aggravated assault. He pleaded guilty to the lesser charge, driving to endanger, was sentenced to six months (which was suspended since he had already been imprisoned for that time), and had his driver’s license suspended for a year. In other words, Smith might legally have been back on the roads during late 2001. King accused the prosecution for having accepted a plea leading to neither jail time nor a permanent revoking of Smith’s license. In a statement read in Oxford County Superior Court, King stated, “What he took from me, my time, my peace of mind and my ease of body, are simply gone and no court can bring them back.”

In an interview on the syndicated entertainment news program *Extra* in October, 1999, Smith complained about feeling unfairly accused of being a bad driver, which he denied in spite of having been sentenced several times for traffic infractions and, according to his own statement, never even saw King, who was six-foot-three, before hitting him. He also claimed that, though he took six different medications, none of them had any impact on his driving, while doctors believed that at least one of them, Valium, was enough to make anyone a worse driver.

In fact, however, Smith never again drove legally. On September 21, 2000, the day of Stephen King's 53rd birthday, Smith died of an accidental overdose. King made a public statement:

"I was very sorry to hear of the passing of Bryan Smith. The death of a 43-year-old man can only be termed untimely. I would wish better for anyone. Our lives came together in a strange way. I'm grateful I didn't die. I'm sorry he's gone."

To make certain that no enthusiastic fan would be able to get hold of it in order to boast of owning the car that nearly killed Stephen King, King bought Smith's 1985 Dodge Caravan for $1,500. Rumor had it that he intended personally to smash it, or to collect money for some charity by letting others break it down for a small fee, but that his wife Tabitha talked him into just having it scrapped.

On the 20th anniversary of his accident, on June 19, 2019, King wrote on Twitter:

"On June 19th, 1999, I got hit by a van while taking a walk. As I lay unconscious in the hospital, the docs debated amputating my right leg and decided it could stay, on a trial basis. I got better. Every day of the 20 years since has been a gift."

And on October 3, 2023, King wrote on X, the new name adopted by Twitter, that he had just had hip surgery as an after-effect of the accident: "I had hip replacement surgery. My right one, crushed in an accident in the summer of 1999, finally gave out."

## Apt Pupil – the film that almost never was

***"That sucker was real good!"***

Some film projects are more problematic than others. One film made from a story by Stephen King has had more than its share of problems: *Apt Pupil*, based on a short story by the same name and initially published in King's collection *Different Seasons*, 1982. The first attempt to film it was made already in 1988. Producer was Richard Korbitz, who had previously filmed two of King's novels, *'Salem's Lot* and *Christine*, in respectively 1979 and 1983; the film was to have been directed by Alan Bridges. The *Apt Pupil* main characters Todd and Dussander were to be played by Ricky Schroder and Nicol Williamson. Initially, the Dussander part was to have been played by James Mason, who had been so memorable in *'Salem's Lot*, but Mason died only a week before Korbitz acquired rights to film the story. When production was launched in 1987, filming commenced and continued for ten weeks – but with eleven days left, money ran out. In 1991, *Cinefantastique* magazine tried to interview Korbitz, who unfortunately declined. The magazine did get to interview William Frye, another producer involved with *Apt Pupil*, but only on condition that the interview would be conducted in writing, and that no discussion was to concern the reasons leading to the film being shelved. These were unusual demands and give rise to wondering if perhaps other than economic problems caused the film's cancellation.

One fact that may have contributed was that when parts of the film were shown to test audiences in Hollywood, Jewish viewers in the theatre hated the movie. The film was very dark, very graphic, and seems to have followed King's story very closely.

When money ran out, Korbitz fought desperately to gain new funding, and was close to succeeding. Both in 1988 and in 1989 it seemed as if the movie might be completed, but sadly neither time proved to work out. In 1991, the money needed suddenly appeared, but by then unfortunately too much time had passed for it to be possible to mix the already finalised scenes with new takes without the audience noticing that the actors had aged. This was particularly noticeable in Rick Schroeder, who played the teenaged Todd Bowden. At the time of initial filming in 1987, Schroeder was 17; by the time money to finish the film was available, he was over 21. With this, the project was finally abandoned, but somewhere between 40 and 75 percent (according to varying sources) of the intended film still exist in more or less final form, and it is far from unreasonable to hope for this to become available at some point. At least one person who has seen it was enthusiastic – and that person is Stephen King himself, who stated, "I got a rough assemblage of about three quarters of the film. Then they ran out of money. And that was good! That sucker was real good!"

No public explanation of why it took more than three years to find someone willing to invest in finishing the film has been given, and it seems clear that Richard Korbitz will never tell us. His only statement on the film was:

"Sadly, Steve may be right about Apt Pupil. My intention was to create a film which incorporated the heart and characterization of The Body with the horror of Stephen King at his most real. It may very well have been the definitive translation of Stephen King into film."

In early 1996, new rumors began circulating about "Apt Pupil" again being about to be filmed. Eight years had passed since the first, failed attempt. This time, Bryan Singer was both producer and director. Todd was now played by Brad Renfro, while Dussander was played by Sir Ian McKellen. *Friends* star David Schwimmer played a supporting role as Edward French, Todd's school guidance counselor. This time, filming was completed on schedule and went into post-production. And then, nothing happened. New problems had turned up. This time, however, not about money, but about nude bodies.

In the film is a dream sequence from a gas chamber in a Nazi concentration camp, where naked young boys are gassed. The parents of some of the children hired as extras for this scene sued TriStar Productions when they learned that their children had been filmed in the nude. Some of the parents also claimed that the film team had told the children that they would be fired unless they agreed to the nude scene, and that this had scared them into complying. If this was true, the company would have committed a crime, since the boys were underage. The claim led to a lengthy legal battle between the production company and the parents, who apparently were not satisfied when the scene was cut from the film. After several months, a judge finally decided to dismiss the suit, since it was impossible to prove the parents' accusations. Additionally, one of the boys publicly stated that he and the others had been told what would happen in the scene, and that any of the extras who were uncomfortable with taking part in the scene could leave the set beforehand.

After this, the upset parents switched tactics and instead, at the end of 1997, began trying to convince others to boycott the film and theatres to refuse showing it. This was however not very effective, and when the producers stated that the gas chamber scene had been refilmed with older actors, a release date of February 1, 1998, was finally set.

But on that date, no film was to be seen. TriStar claimed that they had decided to move the film's opening to the Fall, since it belonged "alongside other more serious-minded films." After an initial opening date of October 1 was again changed, the film finally opened on October 23, 1998, and in the end, *Apt Pupil* was a critical and commercial disappointment.

# The Fourth Decade

## 2004–2014
## *The Tower is reached.*

Possibly the most significant event during Stephen King's fourth decade as a full-time writer happened already at the start of it, on September 21, 2004, and I'm not talking about the fact that on that day he celebrated his 57th birthday. Instead, what I refer to is that his birthday coincided with the official publication date for the seventh and last volume in his "Dark Tower" series, this time also named *The Dark Tower*.

After his 1999 accident, King decided that it was time to finish what he had started when he published his short story "The Gunslinger" in the October 1978, issue of *The Magazine of Fantasy and Science Fiction*. And now, 26 years, seven books and one novella later, it was all done. (Or, perhaps, not quite; in 2012, he published a further book that fit in with the series and was called *The Wind Through the Keyhole*. But since it recounts two stories of Roland's early adventures, which he tells his companions during a storm that occurs between books four and five of the main sequence, and since this interlude does not directly influence their main quest for the Tower, the series can still be viewed as finished when the seventh volume was published.)

With the publication of *The Dark Tower*, Stephen King had concluded a story created over a span of 34 years (King says that he began to work on the first stories already in 1970) and as published in book form filled more than 4,300 pages. Many of even his most enthusiastic readers had no idea of what to make of it. King's ending to his huge story is both frustrating and brilliant. Personally, I admit to not liking it at all when I first read it, but after pondering, it gradually dawned on me that the ending we were given was the only absolutely right one: the only end to the story that would make it whole.

Apart from the two "Dark Tower" books mentioned, Stephen King published a further fifteen books from 2004 to 2014. Among them we find King's own favorite, *Lisey's Story*, his huge novel of the Kennedy assassination, time travel, and alternate history, *11/22/63*, and his sequel to *The Shining*, *Doctor Sleep* (2013). By the end of this decade, King had published a total of 70 books.

## Working with a King: Stewart O'Nan

***"I said I'd write it only if Steve could be my co-author."***

Stephen King readers first heard of Stewart O'Nan in 1997, when he was about to publish a novel called *Dear Stephen King*. The book is written as the autobiographical confession of death row inmate Marjorie Standiford, also called the Speed Queen. She tells all to a tape recorder, hoping that a never-named writer (who is, however, identified as the author of novels called *Misery*, *The Shining*, and *Desperation*) will write her story. Before publication, however, O'Nan's title was changed to *Speed Queen*, after Stephen King's lawyers had objected to the proposed title. In view of this, many of King's readers were surprised when Stephen King and O'Nan seven years later published a co-written nonfiction book about the Red Sox baseball team's 2004 season, which ended with the team winning the World Series for the sixth time, after a hiatus of 86 years since its last previous win. Given this, I decided to get in touch with Stewart O'Nan to talk about his cooperation with Stephen King.

**Lilja:** How is the work with *Faithful* going? I›m guessing that you had a lot of work to do in the last weeks since it›ll be out in about a week, right? Was it your or the publisher's choice to put it out so soon after The Red Sox won The World Series?

**Stewart O'Nan**: *Faithful* is done, or at least it's at the printer's. We had expected all along to have the book in stores by early December, no matter how the team did. The fact that they played all the way till October 27th made us work a little harder, but it was definitely worth it. And the publishers, realizing they now had an even more special book, decided to move the publication date up to November 22nd. But Steve and I both work quickly and cleanly, and they counted on that.

**Lilja:** How happy were you and Stephen when they won? It's almost too good to be true that they won the same year you decide to write a book about them, right?

**Stewart O'Nan**: It's still a bit of a dreamy feeling. Remember, the Red Sox hadn't won the World Series for 86 years. Whole generations of Sox fans never got to see them win it all. Steve thought he'd never see it in his lifetime. So now, when I'm just sitting somewhere doing something, I'll remember: "Oh yeah, the Red Sox won the World Series," and I can't help but smile.

**Lilja:** How did it happen that you and Stephen decided to write the book?

**Stewart O'Nan**: Steve and I have been going to games together for years. We email and talk about the team all the time, and last year in August when the team got hot, Steve decided we should keep a log of our reactions to their games. This spring, when the season was about to start, my agent asked if I wanted to write a book about the Red Sox (every year he asks me this, but this year I'd just finished a novel and finally had the time). I said I'd write it only if Steve could be my co-author. Steve was busy, but said he'd try to contribute as much as he could. And once the season got going, his natural love for the game kicked in and he couldn't stay away.

**Lilja:** How is the book written? Was it hard to write with someone else compared to write alone?

**Stewart O'Nan**: The book is in a double diary format. For each game or Sox-related issue that we found interesting, we'd write separate entries. There are also email exchanges on hot topics. Essentially, the book is a season-long conversation between two supremely interested fans.

Working with another writer--in this case--was easy, since, as fans, we basically agree about what's important. In drafting pieces about players or the games, there was some overlap, but in those cases I'd just edit out any redundancies.

**Lilja:** Is this your first collaboration?

**Stewart O'Nan**: No, I once wrote a screenplay about the life of Clara Schumann with novelist A. Manette Ansay. That was much more difficult, as we didn't quite agree on the role of Brahms or her many children in her life.

**Lilja:** On the first two covers for the book it said «Stewart O'Nan with Stephen King" and not "Stewart O'Nan and Stephen King"? Now, on the final cover, it only lists both your names. Can you explain why that was? Did you write the majority of the book?

**Stewart O'Nan**: I'm not quite sure why they have our names that way, other than that's what the publisher wanted for stocking purposes (that is, how it's listed in bookstores' computers). I'm not sure what the word- or page-count is, but I can safely say I wrote a majority of the text.

**Lilja:** I remembered that you wrote a book you wanted to call *Dear Stephen King* (later renamed *Speed Queen*) some years ago. I then heard (don't know if it's true) that Stephen wouldn't let you use his name in the title. Is that correct and if so, did he give you a reason? And now you're writing a book with Stephen King. Are there no hard feelings about the *Dear Stephen King*-title?

**Stewart O'Nan**: Yes, the whole *Speed Queen* flap was over using Steve›s name, and now that I›ve spent time with him, I see why. Everyone wants a piece of him. So no, there are no hard feelings. He's a prince of a guy, very giving.

**Lilja:** Why did you use Stephen›s name when you wrote *Speed Queen* and not just some fictional name? Were / are you a fan of his books?

**Stewart O'Nan**: I used the name because it made sense to me that, to my character, Stephen King would be the only person who would understand her. He's a confessor-judge figure for her, and for all of America. He understands our deepest hopes and fears (or so she hopes!). And yes, I'm a huge fan of his work, always have been. Without his work--and Ray Bradbury's--I would have never become the reader and writer (the person) I am.

**Lilja:** I heard some time ago that Christina Ricci was going to star in and direct a movie version of *Speed Queen*. What happened to that project?

**Stewart O'Nan**: Christina Ricci was supposed to direct and star in the movie version of *Speed Queen* but could never make time in her schedule to make that happen. As it turned out, she ended up playing a similar role in *Monster*, so I sometimes wonder if she was just blocking our project to make sure it didn't get in the way of that one. *Speed Queen* apparently will get done, as the option was just exercised.

**Lilja:** Do you think there is any chance Stephen will play himself in the movie if it›s ever done?

**Stewart O'Nan**: The screenplays that I've seen don't even deal with that aspect of the book. I think the flap over the title scared the producers.

As a small postscript to this interview, eight years after *Faithful* was published, in 2012, another "collaboration" between King and O'Nan was released as an e-book and an audiobook. *A Face in the Crowd* is a fairly long short story about a man watching baseball on his TV who suddenly begins seeing the faces of dead people once close to him in the audience at the game. King describes this idea already in *Faithful*, then later again mentioned it when speaking at the Savannah Book Festival in early 2012, adding that he didn't know how the story ended, and said to his audience, "I'm gonna give this story to you, you guys write it." Stewart O'Nan was in that audience, and accepted King's challenge. A print version of the story was finally published in the summer of 2023.

# A travelogue: Meeting Stephen King in London, 2006

*"Is your hand tired?"*

December 7, 2006, was the day when it would finally happen. The day when I would at last, after reading Stephen King for 23 years, meet the man who had entertained and enthralled me for so long. King would be in London to promote his new novel, *Lisey's Story*, and I would be there with my friend Anders. We would spend four days in the city, and with a little luck I would see King on at least three of those days.

It all started at 3AM on November 7, when Anders picked me up in his car and we began our journey. The drive to Skavsta Airport took two hours, the flight from there to London only a little over one, then Stansted Express to Liverpool Street Station, the underground to Euston Square, a walk to our hotel on Gower Street. Finally, there, we put our luggage in our rooms and hurried to the Borders bookstore on Oxford Street, where Stephen King would have his first signing.

During the trip I had been in touch with friends in London, who we had hoped might save us places in the line to the event. However, they told us that each customer would be given a number ticket when buying a copy of *Lisey's Story*, and that the number on you ticket would be your place in line for the signing. So, we simply had to hope to be in time.

Around eleven we arrived, bought a book each and received our numbers, #197 and #198. The signing took place on the third floor, but on the second we were stopped by a clerk who told us that the third floor was full. What would that mean? Would we be unable to even see King? But we were quickly relieved by the clerk, who told us that the last person to be allowed up had held the #193 ticket, and that there was no doubt we would make it upstairs. Time passed, the line grew, and at one o'clock, when the signing began, around 150 people were waiting on the second floor. Finally, we were let up, to discover that close to two hundred people were still in line before us – something we probably should have expected, given the numbers on our tickets. Still, far away, in the furthest corner of the floor, we could see a man writing at a table. The King was in the house.
The line moved surprisingly fast and suddenly it was our turn. I went first while Anders took a few photos while I managed a very lame and brief conversation:

**King**: Hi, how are you?
**Lilja**: Fine, and you?
**King**: Fine.

**Lilja**: Is your hand tired?
**King**: No,it's OK, it's on autopilot.

Not my most memorable conversation, and asking if his hand was tired, I can only ascribe to sheer nervousness – but who cares. I had finally met Stephen King!

Next it was Anders' turn, and I was to take his picture with King just as he had taken mine, but no way, José. The attendant had no patience with any delays and simply pushed me away to expedite things. I seem to remember getting a single out-of-focus photo, but luckily there would be other opportunities during our days in London.

Afterwards, it was hard to truly acknowledge what we had experienced. Had we really met Stephen King? Had he really signed our books? Well, his signature really was there, and so was at least the photo Anders had taken of me with King.

Before the evening's event at Battersea Park Event Arena, we returned to our hotel to freshen up. By then we had been traveling for more than twelve hours. A few hours later we left the bus that had brought us to Battersea Park. The only problem was that we had ended up at the wrong edge of the park and could find no signs of either King nor any other of his admirers. But fairly quickly we found the Arena and could join the line with our British friends, who had kept places for us.

After a while we were let in – into a foyer. We waited for another while and were then let into the hall where King would be interviewed and read from his new novel. Our British friends were very dissatisfied with the hall itself, with the very simple chairs provided, and not least with the fact that an airplane lane passed right over the building and provided us with constant noise. But personally, I was mainly filled by wonder over actually being there.

The evening's host entered the stage and told us that he would begin by interviewing Stephen King, who would then take a short pause and after that read from *Lisey's Story*. King came out on stage and was met by applause and cheering worthy of a major rock star. King joked about the size of the audience and said to his host, "We'd be in trouble if they attacked …"

Afterwards we felt that King had given an excellent interview. Only seldom does he give any new information at this kind of public appearance, but this time he told us for the first time that his original title for *Misery* had been *Annie Wilkes's First Edition* and that he had intended to let the story end with Paul Sheldon being eaten by pigs, after which Annie would have bound his book manuscript in his own skin. What was most interesting, however, was that King said that he had found an old book manuscript, written in 1973, which he had decided to publish under his Richard Bachman pen name. In other words, a novel written before even *Carrie* was published! We guessed that this book must be *Blaze*, of which there had been rumors, but King gave no title. That would come later.

After the interview followed a second signing session. We had seats fairly close to where the line would be formed, but what the arrangers had forgotten to plan for was that people went crazy trying to get ahead and any semblance of order immediately collapsed. The idea was that everyone should follow the ”chutes” formed by ropes, but no one even tried. I just managed to slip under the last rope before a guard arrived to restore order. Anders was less lucky and had to spend a little longer than I in line, but if nothing else this meant that I had time to find a place where I would be able to take his picture together with King, since I had failed to do it earlier in the day. Then came the time for my second meeting with King, and if the first one had been short, this one was infinitesimally brief. An assistant took my book, opened it and sent it on to King who signed it, handed it to a next assistant who closed it and gave it back to me. Even so, though, I had been eye to eye with Stephen King for the second time in a single day. With that the day ended, but we felt satisfied in knowing it to have been a really good one.

On day two, November 8, it was time to party. Via contacts at King's British publisher, Hodder & Stoguhton, I had been invited to a publisher's party which King would attend. Dressed in ”slacks and jacket,” as the invitation had read, we left our hotel at around five-thirty.

The venue was Middle Temple, initially part of the headquarters of the Knights Templar until the order was dissolved in 1312. Since 1346, the premises have housed lawyers, and construction on the Hall itself began in 1562. The first recorded performance of William Shakespeare's play *Twelfth Night* took place in the Hall, on February 2, 1602. We knew that we had arrived at the correct building since a car hidden behind the cover of the British edition of *Lisey's Story* was parked outside. Inside, we were shown to the ”gentlemen's cloakroom,” where we were supposed to leave any outer garments.

We did as bid, grabbed free drinks and joined the party. The Hall itself might as well have been part of Hogwarts school for magicians as part of the Inns where the barristers of Britain are trained and to which they belong. Fairly soon it also became obvious that "slacks and jacket" had been only a recommendation, not a demand. We were obviously among the best dressed in the room. But who cares when you attend the same party as Stephen King. And come to think of that, where was he?

While wandering the room looking for King, we found a table full of copies of *Lisey's Story* and of small boxes. We suspected that these perhaps were intended as gifts to those attending, but didn't want to make fools of ourselves, so we waited. When we had seen several others take books and boxes from those offered, we decided to do the same and took a couple of books and boxes each. We later discovered that the boxes contained paperweights manufactured in a limited edition of 500.

Suddenly I saw Stephen King at the opposite end of the room. Dressed in jeans and a t-shirt. No hysteria surrounded him, and perhaps Anders and I were the only ones present who were actually fans of his. To everyone else, this might be just a pleasant part of a normal workday. No matter: gradually we began working our way towards him. What we hoped for this evening was to get the chance of having a few words with him, and perhaps take a good photo.
We got closer and ended up behind King. It became obvious that a woman was guiding him around and introducing people to him. I suspected she might be my contact person at his publisher, but I had no idea of how she might look; we had communicated only via email. I caught her attention, and as it turned out she was not the one I had exchanged mails with, but she knew that I was supposed to be there and asked me and Anders if we wanted to say hello to King. If we did? Of course, we did! After that, everything happened

very fast. The woman said something to King and pointed at us. King turned slightly and looked at us. After that –

> **The woman**: [something I could hear …] "Sweden!"
> **King**: "Ah, from Sweden!"

Anders and I gave our names and shook hands with King. King said that he found himself badly dressed compared to everyone else present but liked that we had adhered to the "slacks and jacket" code.

King: "But you look good, you have a European gangster look going on, like The Sopranos …"

We laughed at this and readied our cameras to take a photo with King, but just as we were ready to do so an Englishman broke in and began talking very fast, introducing his girlfriend to King. Aren't the British supposed to be extremely polite? This one wasn't. But I wouldn't let him spoil this for us. I broke in by asking King if he would pose for a picture. "Sure!" he said. Perhaps he too was tired of the babbling Englishman. Saying that it felt surreal to stand next to King is putting it mildly, but I did, and Anders photographed us. Then we switched and I took a photo of Anders and King. King then disappeared into the crowd and the moment was past. Not even today we feel certain of how long a time we actually spent with King, but filled with happiness over those perhaps three minutes we went outside to cool off and take a look at the photos we had taken. Miraculously, neither one of us, nor Stephen King, had blinked.

Back inside at the party, we noticed that King was moving towards the small scene where the band was playing, and suddenly the singer began putting his name in the song and finally King himself entered the scene and improvised a song. It was all quite surreal, but at the same time highly appreciated and King was rewarded with strong applause.

After the band had stopped playing, and the head of Hodder & Stoughton introduced him, King again went on stage and gave a short thanks to his publisher for the visit they had arranged for him. Background music began to play from the speakers, and one of the tunes was the theme from *The Sopranos*, which felt fitting, giving King's earlier comment to us. It became evident that King was leaving the party. People armed with books and hoping to get them signed were lining his way, but in vain. It had already been made clear that King would do no signings during the evening, and he held to that.

We went towards the exit, hoping possibly to get the chance of exchanging a few more words with King, when we spotted a woman, we had seen earlier, while King spoke, and I felt fairly confident that she must be the Kerry I had been in touch with at Hodder & Stoughton. Suddenly I heard someone address her as Kerry and felt certain about it. Quickly stuck my hand out and introduced myself; happily, she was glad to see me in the flesh. A moment later, King approached, Kerry for the second time introduced me to him and for the second time that evening I shook hands with him.

**Lilja**: It's a real honor to finally meet you.
**King**: It's an honor to meet you.

And with those words, Stephen King left the party, which nevertheless kept going for quite a while. Luckily, we stayed on, and before the evening ended, we had also met Robin Furth, King's research assistant as well as both the author of *The Dark Tower: A Concordance* (2012) and largely responsible for the Marvel graphic novel adaption of the "Dark Tower" series of books. I introduced myself and Robin gave me a huge smile, as happy as I was to finally meet in real life. She then gave us an advance look at the coming graphic novel adaption of Roland's quest for the Tower, and it was fascinating to know that Anders and I were among the first outside of those working on the project to actually see some of it. Then the party ended, and with it another fabulous day.

On Thursday, November 9, it was time to attend a press conference. On the preceding evening, a contact at Hodder & Stoughton had told me that they had invited too many journalists, and that perhaps the room would not hold all of them. Since I obviously had no intention of being one of those unfortunates, I made sure to arrive at ten-thirty in the morning instead of at eleven, when we had been told to arrive in order for everything to be set up by 11:30, when King himself would show up. I was the third to arrive, and so could choose where to sit. Naturally I picked a chair in the front row, as it turned out just six or seven feet from the chair where King himself was seated. Then I waited.

While I waited, I had time to talk a little to other journalists. Among others, I spoke for a while to a few representatives of Sweden's largest morning newspaper, *Dagens Nyheter*, and to a representative of King's Polish publisher. I also again met Kerry from Hodder & Stoughton.

Then it was time. Almost exactly at 11:30 King entered, and people immediately began madly taking pictures. It had been announced that the press conference would begin with a two- minute long photo opportunity, and I have to say that I admire King's patience. He stood there smiling while perhaps 25 or 30 photographers clicked incessantly so that the room seemed full of lightning.

Then came the press conference itself. Everyone present could ask King anything – ”no matter how stupid,” as he himself expressed it.

Personally, I had already decided to try asking more about the new "Richard Bachman" novel King had mentioned during his reading in Battersea Park. I felt that now that I had the chance to ask him something, I wanted to avoid the questions everyone else would ask, and in addition I was very curious about the new Bachman novel. Anders and I had already talked about it, and I wanted once and for all to ask King to confirm that Anders had been right and that the book to come was really *Blaze*.

Unfortunately, many of the questions asked during the press conference were the same as are always asked of Stephen King. For instance, a Russian lady asked King what scares him most. King replied that until the day before, it had been George W. Bush. King was referring to the US midterm election, which the Republican Party, much to King's delight, had lost. King also said that his first thought on learning that Secretary of Defense Donald Rumsfeld has resigned from his position had been, "Ding Dong, the witch is dead."

Stephen King also told us that author Scott Landon's study (in *Lisey's Story*) is modelled on his own, and that his wife Tabitha has a huge influence on his books. One example he gave of this was that in his first version of the ending of *Carrie*, the protagonist simply ran away from the school dance, crying. But his editor wanted there to be more of a disaster, and Tabitha encouraged him to write the one which is now in the novel. He also mentioned that she had absolutely forbidden him to use his original title, "Cancer," for his 2001 novel *Dreamcatcher*.

Time was passing and I felt that I had better put my own question to King. Then we were told that there was time left for only two further questions. I stared frantically at the lady next to King, who picked those who were allowed to ask their questions. After a moment I made eye contact with her, and she nodded back, almost imperceptibly. In that second, I realised that I, Hans-Åke Lilja, will ask a question directly of Stephen King. But there is no time for further thought; the lady beside King points to me and says, "Last question, right here."

Someone puts a microphone before me and I say, "Hans Lilja from Lilja's Library. At the Battersea Park reading you mentioned a new Bachman book; can you tell us more about it?" King repeated roughly what he had said at his reading: that he had found the manuscript in his basement, that it was written in 1973, that it is a crime novel and needs updating, but that he considers it a quite good novel. But he never mentioned a title, so before the session was ended, I asked, "Does it have a title?", and King replied, "Yes, *Blaze*."

With that, the press conference ended. Now King would sign books and other items someone might want to have signed. Unbelievably, several attendants just rose and left. How can someone decline such an opportunity, even if they aren't actual fans? Most, however, got in line for a few further seconds with Stephen King, and of course I was one of them. When I got to the head of the line, I held out my ticket from the Battersea reading, which I wanted to have signed. "Ah, you were there?" King said. When he had signed my ticket, I took a chance and held out my invitation for the preceding evening's party to get his signature on that as well. But when I asked him to sign it, King said, "No, but I can sign that one", and reached for my copy of *Lisey's Story*, which had been handed out to everyone at the press conference. I have no idea of why he wouldn't sign the invitation, but perhaps he knew that the paper it was printed on was so glossy that his signature would smudge, or perhaps he believed I would sell it on eBay. No matter: I was more than satisfied.

But I would have to wait to savor what I had just experienced. I was already late for the next event, for King was scheduled to sign books at the Asda Supercentre in Watford at five P.M., the time was already half an hour past noon, and I was in a hurry. I quickly walked to the nearest underground station to get to the train station where I would catch my train to Watford Junction, and from there I spent another ten minutes in a cab to the Asda store. No trip is too complicated when you're on your way to a Stephen King signing, I smilingly observed.

When I arrived, my first thought was that this was a typical discount store, and I wondered why they had felt it reasonable to send King out here to do a signing – the store was in the middle of nowhere, and hadn't even bothered to stock up on any King books apart from *Lisey's Story*. Which was unfortunate in my case. I hadn't brought along any book of my own to get signed, since at the earlier signing you first had to buy a book to get a signing ticket. Here, this was not the case, and so I would have preferred to get some other book signed – but no such luck, since there were no others to be had. So, I bought another copy of *Lisey's Story*, my last of the five – four of which were signed – I brought back from England.

Again, my British friends had kept a place in line for me, and I was now the 35th person in line to get my book signed. The line wasn't particularly long and some of us talked of perhaps getting back in at the end of it after having our first books signed. But with around an hour to go, a huge number of others began getting in line and we dismissed that notion. When King began signing, I would estimate that at least some six hundred people were in line.

While standing in line I recognized a man whom I had previously seen both at the Borders signing, the reading, the party, and the press conference. I assumed that he must have something to do with King, and it turned out that I was right; he was from Hodder & Stoughton, and a little later came up to talk to us. He was more than nice and told us that he had designed both the paperweights handed out at the party and the bookmarks that had been given out at the British book release. Only 500 paperweights had been produced, while the bookmark had been printed in 5,000 copies.

Then it was suddenly five o'clock and King appeared. Previously one of my English friends and I had agreed to switch cameras so that we could each have a photo of having our books signed by King, but before reaching the head of the line, to our surprise, we were told that no photos would be allowed. Luckily, however, there was instead a woman who took Polaroid photos of each person as King signed their books. Not a bad idea, though the Polaroid pictures were far from first-rate.

When my turn came, I had intended to ask King to sign a small poster I had brought along from the press conference, but the lady standing just where we came up to the table told us that he would only sign copies of *Lisey's Story*. I can't understand why; after all I had evidently bought a copy of the book. Someone else had only a copy of *The Colorado Kid*, and again the lady objected. But this time King himself said that he was perfectly happy to sign that novel and did so – the King had spoken. At any rate, I handed him my copy of *Lisey's Story*, and he signed it. I said, "Thank you," and put out my hand, but at the same moment King took his glass of Coca-Cola from the table and total confusion occurred. But King quickly recovered and reached out his left hand, which I shook. Which meant that by now I had shaken both King's right and left hand and felt as totally satisfied as only a true nerd can feel.

Then all that remained was the long journey back. When I arrived at my hotel it struck me that apart from breakfast, all I had eaten during the day was two Big Cats and a few swallows of Coca-Cola, but who cares? On days like that one, there were more important things to do than eating.

The last day of the trip was set aside for the return trip to Sweden, and the only thing related to Stephen King was when I was passing customs and was stopped and searched. Of course, I became worried when the customs official began checking my books. I asked her to handle them carefully, and when she saw that they were signed copies, she said, "I'm not worthy of holding the same books as Stephen King." The books were fine, and four days in November 2006, which I will never forget were ended.

# Publishing books about Stephen King

***They didn't really believe that Hans-Poop Lilja would sell.***

Have you ever thought about how it would feel to be the editor of a book containing a story by Stephen King? How it would feel to have your name along with that of Stephen King on the cover of a book? I never had before 2008, but in that year, something happened that would start a ball rolling that in the end would lead also to the book you hold in your hands right now, more than fifteen years later.

Back in 2008, I unexpectedly heard from *Cemetery Dance*, an American publishing company founded in 1988 by Richard Chizmar and specialising in horror and dark suspense. They asked me whether I had ever considered publishing my website "Lilja's Library – The World of Stephen King" in book format. My completely honest reply was, "No." My reaction was to wonder why anyone would want to buy a book containing material available for free on the Internet. *Cemetery Dance* begged to disagree, claiming that there was a market for books like that and suggesting that they would be happy to give it a try. Who was I to disagree with a successful publisher? And besides, I thought it a very cool idea – who, in all honesty, wouldn't like to have their work presented for posterity in a physical book? So, the decision was made to publish *Lilja's Library: The World of Stephen King – The Book*, and work on it began. One early decision was to include the interviews I had conducted for my website, and to add a number of new ones made exclusively for the book. On April 15, 2009, the book was announced as available for pre-orders, and no one was more proud than I. I was about to have a book published.

When published, the book contained an introduction by Bev Vincent, who is a leading expert on Stephen King; an interview with me; my Stephen King interviews and a further 38 interviews with persons in some way connected to Stephen King; no less than 175 reviews and an afterword, in all a book of 512 pages. It was also illustrated by Glenn Chadbourne, who also drew the first rendering of Marv, the Lilja's Library mascot, who also had the honor of appearing on the cover of the book.

The book was published in two formats: as a trade hardcover priced at $40, and as a limited and boxed edition of 52 numbered copies, signed by me and priced at $250 – which I thought of as totally absurd: Nobody would buy it, not even my parents. Nor did they – that is, my parents didn't. Others, it seemed, did: the limited edition, which I doubted anyone would even consider buying, was sold out three weeks before publication, which was on August 3, 2010.

Before then, however, reading copies had been sent out already in late 2009, and to my delight *Fangoria*, the leading horror film magazine, in its issue #289 for December 2009, selected my book as its "book of the month." My pride was limitless. More reviews followed, most of them on the whole positive, and Mike Perkins and Laura Martin, who had created the graphic novel version of *The Stand*, had a number of fictional King characters ask about their appearances in a humorous brief comic strip.

Less than two years after the book's publication, in May 2012, *Cemetery Dance* informed me that it was sold out, which again made me proud – my publisher's gamble had paid off. For those perhaps interested, it is however still available as an e-book. Looking back at the book today, I must admit to doing it both with pride and with some shame. Unfortunately, it could have been better. The earliest of the reviews in it are by now around 25 years old, and I have to admit that back then I was hardly as good a writer as I imagined. Hopefully I have learned since, and today I trust that I do better. But even so, damn it, it remains *my* book. My first book, and of course I am proud of it!

On August 9, 2012, *Cemetery Dance* began advertising my second book, written in cooperation with Brian James Freeman and Kevin Quigley. The book is called *The Illustrated Stephen King Movie Trivia Book* and the *Cemetery Dance* marketing stated:

"Today Cemetery Dance are pleased to announce *The Illustrated Stephen King MOVIE Trivia Book* by Brian James Freeman, Kevin Quigley, and Hans-Ake Lilja, which features more than 1,000 questions about the movies, miniseries, and television episodes based on ideas conjured from the imagination of the King of Horror, along with more than 50 illustrated questions created by Glenn Chadbourne and an exclusive afterword by Mick Garris, director of The Stand, The Shining, Riding the Bullet, Desperation, Bag of Bones, and many others!"

As the text states, the book contains more than a thousand questions about feature films and TV serials based on Stephen King stories. All three of us worked hard on making up questions. If memory serves, Kevin managed to come up with the greatest number of questions, while I sorted them up and kept track of them, and Brian did all the practical matters that have to be handled when you intend to publish a book. We worked well together, and it was a gratifying experience, even if from my point of view, it was more of an administrative task than one of writing a book.

The book was published on September 20, 2013, and this time in three formats: as a softcover selling at $19,95, a hardcover selling for

$40, and a signed, limited edition priced at $300. Again, the book sold out in all formats.

After this second outing, two years passed before I began thinking about a further book. Again, *Cemetery Dance* was my publisher, and in fact the specific idea for the book was given me by Brian James Freemantle who had been one of my co-authors for *The Illustrated Stephen King Movie Trivia Book*. He was now the managing editor of *Cemetery Dance*, and when I told him that I wanted to do something special to celebrate the first twenty years of "Lilja's Library – The World of Stephen King," he suggested that I put together a collection of stories celebrating Stephen King – an anthology of stories by authors with some kind of connection to King. Perhaps a bit overly bold I stated that a story by King himself was necessary, and with that said the first step had been taken on the road to what would become *Shining in the Dark*, a book that would come to mean very much more than I could even have guessed at when I had that decisive conversation with Brian.

That conversation with Brian took place in 2015, and the idea was for the book to be published in 2016, when my web page celebrated its 20th anniversary. Unfortunately, that didn't happen, and mainly due to the fact that I was much too optimistic about the time needed to finish a book with a number of authors involved. It took time to send out invitations to those I hoped to have stories from, it took time for them to reply, if they replied at all. It took time to negotiate both fees and fitting stories. Some cases were simpler than others, some very difficult, but in the end, I had managed to gather my dream team, where two of the authors stood out more than the others.

The first of them was of course Stephen King himself. After a number of back and forth mailing, I was at last allowed to pick one of the stories on my wish list, and in the end, I picked "The Blue Air Compressor." Already from the start I had wanted to use an older story which King had chosen not to include in any of his own collections. Partly because I wanted to showcase his early style, partly also for the practical reason that if King had chosen not to include the story in any collection of his, the risk of him doing so in the future was small. A newly written story would probably have been unique to my anthology only until his next own collection was published, while an older story would probably never appear anywhere else. And if William Thompson, King's Doubleday editor, gets the last word, I will be right in this. In a letter to King dated April 22, 1977, Thompson discussed which stories should be included in the then still not finalised collection *Night Shift*, published in 1978. Thompson wrote:

"Now we should start talking about the stories. There are some that are excellent and some that are too much "Steve-the-student-writer." And I think we should be selective, at this point in your career, about including the early not-so-good ones. These could, I feel, do you more harm than good and I hope you'll agree."

Thompson then went on specifically about "*The Blue Air Compressor.*"

"It's a precious author talk for one thing and also distasteful. It doesn't come close of being a take-off of horror fiction. Let's keep it in the drawer."

King accepted Thompson's wish and the story was never included in any of his collections, though it had originally been published in the January 1971, issue of *Onan*, the literary magazine of the University of Maine, and a revised version was later published in *Heavy Metal* magazine for July 1981. Consequently, when my anthology was published the story had not been available to readers for 37 years. I well remember when I was granted permission to reprint it. I and my family were in London and spent an evening in our hotel room when the email arrived. To be exact, it arrived on Friday evening, July 17, at 8:30 P.M.

The other short story in the book that has meant much to me is ”The Keeper's Companion” by John Ajvide Lindqvist. After my initial query, he replied that he thought the idea intriguing, but that he was just about to publish a new short story collection called *Våran hud, vårat blod, våra ben* (2016 in Sweden; the title translates as *Our Skin, Our Blood, Our Bones*), and so had no unpublished short stories on hand, but that he would get back in touch if he happened to come up with some good story idea. That sounded fine, but to be completely honest I believed at the time that what he gave me was his standing reply: I simply assumed that he had more requests than stories, and that this was the answer whenever someone asked him for a contribution. But I quickly learned that I had completely misread him, for after only a couple of weeks I had a new email from John, who now wrote:

What do you know? I'm now writing a short story which seems quite promising. It's about a group of kids who play ”Call of Cthulhu” and is connected to that universe. I think I will call it ”The Keeper's Companion.”So maybe I will contribute after all!

And he did. A little over a month later I received another email with an attached Word document that contained ”The Keeper's Companion.” And as a bonus, five years later I got to know him better on a personal basis, after having asked him if perhaps he wanted a hand in handling his official website, which at the time seemed quite static. I felt that he deserved a better online presence, and it all lead to the fact that since 2020, I'm moonlighting as John's webmaster. So, it goes.

Let's get back to my anthology. The original idea, as I've already mentioned, was that it should be published in 2016 when my website "Lilja's Library – The World of Stephen King" would celebrate its first twenty years, and in October 2016, *Cemetery Dance* announced the book as forthcoming. By now it had a fabulous cover painted by Vincent Chong, who by now had also updated the "Marv" character. Working with Vincent on the cover was a fabulous experience; this is how he described it on his web page:

"Lilja and I worked closely together to come up with the idea for the cover art. He wanted an image that reflected 'Lilja's Library' but would not only just appeal to fans of the site. One image that kept coming to him was that of a man or creature sat looking at a computer screen with something scary about him. I thought this was a great starting point, and furthermore that the creature should be the website's mascot Marv (originally created by Glenn Chadbourne). I liked the setting of a creepy 'library' room and further tied it in with the website by having the banner appear on the computer screen. Early on, Lilja suggested maybe using imagery from the Stephen King story for the cover; while we veered away from that idea, I did manage to include a nod to it by making it look like Marv was reading the story on the screen."

Unfortunately delays made the book late. 2016 ended and 2017 began. On January 24, I received a Messenger note I had never even imagined might happen to me – a Bulgarian lady named Vesela had learned of my forthcoming anthology, worked for a publishing company named Pleiad, and asked whom to contact regarding Bulgarian rights to the book. In a cold sweat and with trembling fingers I replied that she could talk directly to me. She told me that Pleiad wanted to publish a Bulgarian translation of my anthology, and without the slightest idea of what I was getting into I replied, "Of course, that'll be fine." And so, it came that the Bulgarian edition of *Shining in the Dark* was published on November 22, 2017, and became the first published edition of the anthology. But the spelling of my name was changed in the book, and I became Hans-Oke Lilja … for the simple reason that "ake" in Bulgarian means "poop," and the publishing house didn't really believe that Hans-Poop Lilja would sell, an assessment I agreed with. In January of 2018 Pleiad also invited me to do a book tour in Bulgaria; I spent three days in Sofia, was interviewed on Bulgarian television, signed books and gave lectures via an interpreter, which was a unique experience. Later in the same month, the *Cemetery Dance* editions of the book were also released, and after that I began wondering whether more countries might perhaps be interested in the book.

It turned out that several were. Already during 2018, the anthology was published in Italy, the Czech Republic, Germany, the UK, and Sweden (to which I'll return). In 2019 followed a translation in Serbia, in 2020 further ones in Brazil, Japan and France, then in 2021 in Greece and Russia, in 2022 in Poland and Spain, finally in Turkey in 2023 and in the Netherlands in 2024. Today the book has been published in 17 languages and in 37 different editions. Imagine if someone had mentioned that in 2015, when Brian and I first began discussing the project.

Back to the Swedish edition. The Swedish title for *Shining in the Dark* is *Varsel i mörkret*, making it one of the title translations that has managed to keep my play on titles. For "shining" obviously is borrowed from Stephen King's novel *The Shining*, which in Swedish translation is called *Varsel* – which makes for my Swedish title *Varsel i mörkret* [literally "Foreboding in the Dark"]. Not bad, I think.

The first Swedish edition was published in 2018 and launched via a Kickstarter campaign, run by me with two small publishing houses, Apart and Swedish Zombie. If anyone happens not to know what a

Kickstarter is, it's a way of selling a book before it exists to generate the money to publish it, a form of grass roots financing. You put up a minimum goal, and if that amount of money is pledged during the time allotted, you publish the book; if not, there is no book. If you get more money pledged than the minimum, you can increase the quality of the book. We put up a minimum goal of 100,000 Swedish crowns (currently around US $10,000), and for that we would have published the book as a quality paperback. In the end we actually got pledges for slightly more than SEK 200,000 and could publish it as a hardcover and with a bonus story by Brian Keene (which is included in only this edition) and with a new cover by Vincent Chong, who also painted the original American cover. The new cover made me more than happy; it's a joy to work with Vincent, who is immensely gifted. What we did with the new cover also had a deeper notion, which we hoped that readers would understand. The painting now depicts the same scene as the earlier cover but viewed from the opposite direction. There are also two books visible in the painting: one is the Swedish edition of Stephen King's *The Shining*, obviously for the reason I just gave concerning the title, the other the original edition of *X*, John Ajvide Lindqvist's 2017 novel. That book is included because John wrote an original story for the anthology, and *X* was picked because one of the characters in it is named Hans-Åke, which I enjoyed. Most of the 666 copies of the book we had printed were pre-sold, and it is now long out of print.

The whole Kickstarter adventure was interesting, and at the time seemed the only way to get the book published, but it also entailed an enormous amount of work. Would I publish a further book via Kickstarter? Maybe.

The problem, though, was that the entire print run was sold out almost immediately after publication, and when readers began discovering its existence there were no longer any copies available.

That made me keep looking for some publisher who would take over and issue a paperback reprint that could meet the demand that had materialized. Every time I read about some publisher I had not previously known of, I sent them a mail describing the book, its content and its history, hoping that they would find it interesting enough to give it a try. Unfortunately, the only replies I got were variations on "Thanks, but your book does not fit our publishing profile," and after a while I began doubting that it would ever be published in any larger Swedish print run. But doubt didn't make me give up, and one day in early December 2019, while surfing on my mobile, I saw a mention of some publisher whose name I have by now forgotten and decided to contact them. I googled their name to find some means of getting in touch, but to my surprise that publisher was only the second choice I got back; the first choice was another publisher unknown to me, Ekström & Garay. I decided to mail both of these new houses, and did so, after which I and my son were to go shopping for some dinner. But before we were even out the door my phone rang. My caller was Melker Garay, publisher at Ekström & Garay, and he wanted to do my book. After fifteen minutes on the phone, it had been decided that Ekström & Garay would publish a new edition of the anthology, and four months later the book had shipped and was put on sale. Chance had struck again, this time in a way almost impossible to imagine.

My cooperation with Ekström & Garay has since then led to first my book *Stephen King: Not Just Horror*, published in 2023, and then to the book you are now reading. My vague notion back in 2008 to perhaps have my website published in book format has in the course of just over fifteen years led to me currently writing my fifth book. A dizzying fact and proof that chance can be something quite wonderful.

# The Fifth Decade

## 2014–2024
### *The Holly decade*

In 2014, Holly Gibney entered the world of Stephen King. She did so as a very special character in his novel *Mr Mercedes* and returned in the two following novels of the Bill Hodges trilogy: *Finders Keepers*(2015), and *End of Watch*(2016). Initially she was intended to be just a minor character, but King became so fond of her that he let her take one of the lead roles in the three books, and by now she is one of the very few characters he has returned to repeatedly. Apart from the three Bill Hodges novels, she has been the protagonist of his novel *The Outsider*(2018), his novelette "If It Bleeds" in the collection by that name (2020), and his novel *Holly*(2023).

So, Stephen King obviously has a weak spot for Holly, but far from all of his readers do. Some boycott the books where she is featured; some buy them to keep their King collections complete but refuse to read them. Absurd? Yes, of course, but that's a par for the King universe. Those living in it hold strong opinions, and there is little or nothing to be done about that.

King himself has said of Holly, "I could never let Holly Gibney go. She was supposed to be a walk-on character in Mr. Mercedes and she just kind of stole the book and stole my heart. *Holly* is all her."

During his fifth decade (2014–2024), Stephen King published 18 books and reached a total of 88. Among those perhaps more notable than others we find his children's book *Charlie the Choo-Choo* (2016) and his novels *The Institute* (2019) and *Billy Summers* (2021).

## Two more pen names

***"If I were ever to write a children's book, it would be just like this!"***

Already in 1972, two years before *Carrie* was published, King used a pen name for his short story "The Fifth Quarter," published in the April issue of *Cavalier* magazine: John Swithen. Swithen was King's first pen name, and the story was the only thing he published under that name. It was later reprinted in his collection *Nightmares & Dreamscapes*, and in his comments to it King wrote, "Bachman again, or maybe George Stark," referring to his established Bachman pen name and to a character in his novel *The Dark Half*, a novel about a pseudonym who refuses to disappear. The Swithen story was also filmed as one of the eight episodes of the TV mini-series *Nightmares & Dreamscapes: From the Stories of Stephen King*, shown on the TNT network.

But since this was the only time King used the John Swithen name, why did he do so long before even his own name had become familiar to readers? I put that question to him when interviewing him in 2007, and he said:

"The Swithen thing ... at that time I was publishing stories all the time in *Cavalier* and this story wasn't like the horror stories. It's this hardboiled crime thing and I had a story in the previous issue and it was really like the pulp writers who used to use all different names in the 50's 'cause they poured that stuff out and that was my time to just pour stuff out so I used the John Swithen name but I never used it again. I didn't really like it."

Time passed, and when the feature film of *The Dark Tower* (2017) was to be marketed at the San Diego Comic Con, the short children's book *Charlie the Choo-Choo* was extracted from *The Dark Tower 3: The Waste Lands* (1991), where it is included in the novel's narrative. It was published as a stand-alone book and carried a cover quote from Stephen King: "If I were ever to write a children's book, it would be just like this!" The book was printed in only 150 copies and used as promotion for the film. In the *Dark Tower* novel its author's name is given as "Beryl Evans," and to make its release more authentic actress Allison Davis from Los Angeles was hired to portray Beryl Evans at the convention, where she also had a signing session. The book immediately became a collector's item and was very difficult to get hold of until its publisher finally reprinted it in a trade edition.

The whole text of *Charlie the Choo-Choo*is is included in *The Dark Tower 3: The Waste Lands*, where it also plays a considerable role. The book also turns up in *The Dark Tower 5: Wolves of the Calla* (2003), but there its author's name is given as Claudia y Inez Bachman instead of Beryl Evans.

When interviewing King in 2007 I also asked if he had ever written under any further pen names, and he denied it. I pushed him a little by asking whether he would tell me if he had done so, and to that he replied, "Actually, at this point I would, but I never have." And I believe him. King is in a position where he can publish whatever he wants to, and as much as he wants to. And indeed, does he really feel a need to publish more than he already does?

## Workingwith a King: Owen King

*"My father agreed."*

Owen King is Stephen King's youngest child. I was lucky enough to visit one of the stops on their joint publicity tour for *Sleeping Beauties* (2017), their co-written novel. This was in New York, and apart from Owen and Stephen King I also met Peter Straub, with whom Stephen King had written *The Talisman* and *Black House* and who I had now a chance to talk briefly with. He also agreed to pose for a photograph with me, taken with my mobile phone by none other than Stephen King.

In September 2017, a few days before the release date for *Sleeping Beauties*, I had the pleasure of interviewing Owen King. This interview is reprinted below. The book Owen King mentions working on at the end of the transcript was probably *The Curator*, published in March 2023.

**Lilja:** I just finished the book *Sleeping Beauties.* A great book that you wrote with your dad, Stephen King. How did the idea that you two should collaborate on the book come about?

**Owen King:** Thank you! I›m glad you enjoyed it. The genesis was just a one sentence pitch that I made to my dad: "What if all the women in the world fell asleep?" I wanted him to take the idea and run with it. The notion struck me as one that you could make a hell of a disturbing meal out of, and that's kind of his specialty, whereas most of my own writing to that point had been pretty mainstream. He was very insistent that I should write it, though. Eventually, we compromised and wrote it together.

**Lilja:** Can you take us through the process of writing the book?

**Owen King:** We just passed it back-and-forth. If I did twenty-five pages, he'd rewrite me and then do his twenty-five. If he did fifty pages, I'd rewrite him, and then I'd do fifty pages. All that rewriting is, for me, central to a positive collaboration. You have to allow your collaborator to take ownership of what you write, and they have to allow you to take ownership of what they write. It also helps unify the voice of the novel.

And we did a clever thing to utterly foil any attempt to determine who wrote what parts: if I was writing a section, I would leave a hole in it for my father to fill in a particular scene that I would suggest, and vice versa.

It's a long book, but I feel like the complete first draft took about ten or eleven months to complete. Neither of us let it sit on a desk too long.

**Lilja:** I heard that it was supposed to be a TV series of 10 episodes and that you wrote the script for the first two episodes before you decided it should be a book instead. What made you change the format from TV series to a book?

**Owen King:** That›s correct. We wrote two episodes and many of the events that occurred in the first two hundred pages of the novel were hammered out there originally. What was great about the scripts was that they helped us figure out the action and really work out how the sleeping sickness would initially play out on a macro level, how the news would spread. Some of the characters emerged quickly, too. I remember that Evie popped off the page right away. We were able to find the right balance of her immediately; she's terrible and bizarrely charismatic and certainly not human, but then again, not entirely inhuman, either.

However, there were other characters that I wanted to explore further, and I felt like the fast-moving narrative that we'd created was pushing them to the edges. So, I suggested that we turn it into a novel and let the whole thing spread out more. My father agreed.

**Lilja:** Do you think that the script version will be published eventually?

**Owen King:** I guess we could show a fragment at some point, but I wouldn't want to publish the two scripts in their entirety. They're just rough drafts now.

I know you were also wondering, on a related note, about what ended up being cut from the first draft of the novel. I'm not sure how it happened, but I sense that there's a vague impression out there that the novel was cleaved in half or something in the midst of the editing process. We probably cut thirty or forty pages of manuscript - not that much in the grand scheme. Ninety percent of those cuts were simply made to sharpen the writing. A certain scene might have had one or two more beats, an extra line of description, that kind of stuff. I can recall two small story elements that got clipped out and that's it. And they were really small things.

**Lilja:** The book contains a lot of characters. How did you keep track of them when you wrote the book?

**Owen King:** At some point we started up a version of the character list that›s at the front of the book. It was a cheat sheet, basically. It included quotes from the draft that explained what each character looked like, their job, their relations, their concerns, and so on. It was pretty elaborate, and we did have a few mix-ups along the way. My dad is an experienced hand at books with huge casts, though, and I'm super anal about details.

**Lilja:** What's the biggest difference in collaborating on a book compared to writing your own book? I guess that there are both pros and cons?

**Owen King:** The best part of a successful collaboration is the constant inspiration and challenge. Your collaborator comes up with some brilliant improvisation, or does a beautiful job with a scene, and you feel compelled to attempt to match what they've done. That happened many times in the writing of *Sleeping Beauties*. My dad's stuff lifted me up and I'd be ultra-focused to maintain that new level that he'd found.

I suppose the great drawback of collaboration is that there is negotiation, and you occasionally have to give up some element because the other person isn't keen on it. That said, we found such a good rhythm, I don't recall that happening too many times. We were thinking a lot of the same thoughts.

**Lilja:** You have written a book, short stories and a comic. How do you look at yourself as a writer?

**Owen King:** I just write. I›m sure I had a sharper vision of who I wanted to be as a writer when I was younger. Whatever story feels most urgent, that's what I work on. It doesn't really matter to me what it is.

**Lilja:** Growing up in a family of writers (mother, brother and father). How did that effect you and your writing?

**Owen King:** My family has influenced me in lots of ways, but the big one is with work ethic. I learned at a young age that you have to be dedicated. If you want to write, you have to do it all the time.

**Lilja:** You're going on tour in September and October to promote *Sleeping Beauties* with Stephen King. What can those of us attending expect?

**Owen King:** I know that we›ll each read a few pages from the book. There will be a Q&A portion. I imagine that there will be, in addition to questions about *Sleeping Beauties*, lots of inquiries for my father about the film adaptation of *It* which will be very fresh.

**Lilja:** What are you working on now and what can we expect from you down the road?

**Owen King:** I wrote the pilot for a TV adaptation of *Sleeping Beauties* for the amazing production duo of Michael Sugar and Ashley Zalta at Anonymous Content. I›m hoping that will turn out to be an on-going project - we shall see. There are some other film-TV projects in the works, too.

A short film I co-wrote with my dear friend Mark Jude Poirier, *Father Daughter Dance*, is going to be playing at the YoFi Festival in November. It's about a handyman having a truly terrible day. Mark directed and he did a superb job. I'm excited for people to see that.

A new short story I'm really proud of will be appearing as a part of the Ploughshares solo series in 2018.

What else? Well, working on a new book. It doesn't have a title yet. I'd say it's a bit more in line with *Sleeping Beauties* than with my previous writing.

**Lilja:** The script for the pilot of the TV adaptation for *Sleeping Beauties* that you wrote, is it very different from the version you and Stephen wrote when you started it all?

**Owen King:** The pilot I wrote is quite different from the original pilot because it's based entirely on the novel.

**Lilja:** With that I'd like to thank you for doing this interview. It was a pleasure to speak to you. Thanks.

# A travelogue: A Kingly meeting in New York

***”To Lilja – all the best – enjoy NCY!”***

It is September 26, 2017, the day when Stephen and Owen King's novel *Sleeping Beauties* is released in the US. It is also the day on which the two Kings begin their promotion tour for the book. A tour that will take them to ten sold-out events in ten different cities. The first of them is New York, and there I am, in the center of the city and ready to watch the Kings.

The day starts early since I am jetlagged and wake up at 3 A.M. But I use the time well and after a shower and breakfast walk down to the studio where *Good Morning America* is recorded. On the day before I learned that Stephen and Owen King would be among today's guests. I ought to have been able to figure that out, since King is

usually a guest on the show when one of his books is released. Getting a ticket is not even worth thinking about, since they are long gone. This doesn't make me particularly disappointed; their guest segment is only a few minutes long, and the rest of the show isn't particularly interesting. Instead, it is much more interesting to stand outside the entrance to the studio and watch the guests arrive. Apart from Stephen and Owen King, this day Harrison Ford and Kate Winslet are also guests, and if Stephen King has many fans,

they are still a drop in the ocean compared to the number of fans here to see Harrison Ford. And in the middle of this throng of fans, professional photographers, autograph hunters and just plain rubberneckers I stand and see Stephen and Owen King arrive in black SUVs looking more or less as the ones featured in the TV series *24.*

After the show is taped and the Kings have left, I wander around Manhattan, stopping for coffee in Central Park with movie reviewer Gunnar Rehlin, the man who taught us everything about movies when I was younger. He too has come to see Stephen and Owen King, though at another time than I. Still, it's hard to focus on other things than what is to happen. I'm not only to see Stephen and Owen King read from their book in front of an audience but have also been invited by Stephen King's assistant Marsha DeFilippo to come behind stage before their reading to say hello to them.

The event doesn't start until 7 P.M., but people begin to line up hours earlier in front of St. Ann & the Holy Trinity Church in Brooklyn

Heights. There are no numbered seats in the church, so whoever comes first will get the best seats, and if you want to sit close to the readers you had better be early in line. I get there around a quarter past six and as agreed phone Marsha. Of course, it would be too easy if she answered on my first try. Instead, I end up in her voice-mail and start to feel panicky. Time is short and everything must come together in order for me to get to meet Stephen and Owen King. But soon contact is established and at six-thirty I am let in via a side door to see Stephen King.

I'd be lying if I claimed that I wasn't nervous, but just as on the previous occasions I had met him, Stephen King is very friendly. I quickly calm down and shake hands with him. He asks me if I like New York, if I have come all the way here just for this event (and seems a bit surprised when I reply, "Yes, I have") and if I am jetlagged. We talk for a short while and I ask him if he might sign my copy of *Sleeping Beauties*, which I had bought earlier in the day just in case some occasion to have it signed might present itself. He obviously had nothing against signing it, and wrote:

To Lilja – all the best – enjoy NCY!
Stephen King
9/26/17

Just after he had signed the book Marsha also took what at least according to me is the best of all photos I have of myself with King. Right then I didn't read what he had written in the book, and only later realised that he had switched the letters so that NYC had turned into NCY. King said, "I'll ask Owen to sign as well," and Owen King not only signed the book but also drew a moth. Moths play a significant part in the story, which was why he picked that particular subject for his drawing.

While Owen King was signing my book, I saw yet another face I recognized. Fairly close to us sat no less a person than Peter Straub, who co-wrote *The Talisman* and *Black House* with Stephen King. I am unable not to take the chance of introducing myself to him. He and I had previously communicated by email, and he remembered me. Now, after the fact, I can't help being a bit annoyed over not having guessed that he would be present. I knew that he lived in New York, and I knew that he and Stephen King like to get together whenever they get a chance. Why didn't I bring a copy of *The Tal-*

*isman* to get it signed by both of them? But at any rate I enjoyed meeting him and having a few words with him. Stephen King also suggested that I should get my photo together with Peter Straub, and even offered to take it, with the result that I now have a photo of myself and Peter Straub by Stephen King. You can even see the shadow of King's finger in the upper left corner, where he happened to hold it minutely in front of the lens. While at it, Stephen King also took a photo of me and his son Owen. And then it was time for the two Kings to make their last preparations for their reading, and for me to move out into the church room.

When I entered the church from the back some people looked strangely at me and probably wondered who I was and why I came in that way and why I held a copy of *Sleeping Beauties*. But nobody said anything.

Just as I came in, I realised that I didn't have a bracelet. Everyone who had bought a ticket to the event received one when entering the church, and after the event when they left, you were expected to hand in your bracelet in exchange for a copy of *Sleeping Beauties*. Also, 400 of the 750 copies of the book that were to be handed out to the audience would be signed. Who received the signed copies was left entirely to chance. Obviously, I didn't want to miss out on this, so I walked up to the entrance, where those handing out bracelets sat, and told them that I hadn't received one since I had come in through the back door and spent some time with the two Kings. Those were not my exact words, but I said something similar and realised that probably nobody would believe me. But they just handed me a bracelet without comment.

Not unexpectedly all the good seats were already taken when I finally began trying to find somewhere to sit, but I noticed that many had found places on a balcony which ran along both sides of the church and went up there to look for a free seat. There was one, in fact in the first row. It was also immediately left of some electric equipment, at a guess some part of the sound system, but who cares? The seat was perfect, and I had a fantastic view of the stage, which was very simple. Two chairs, two posters showing the book cover, Stephen and Owen King. Nothing more. Stylish and clean.

The event was introduced by Emma Straub (who also asked her father to stand, and the audience cheered), and then the two Kings entered.

Stephen and Owen King each read from their novel. After their reading they asked each other questions, which they said they had prepared without showing them to each other. It turned into an interesting and spontaneous discussion. Among other things we learn that Owen King used to put his G. I. Joe figures in the freezer and that together they had created a G. I. Joe figure. They spoke about how they cooperated on the novel, about Owen when younger having recorded audiobooks for his father and how to best keep your characters apart and avoid repeating them.

At the end, they opened for questions from the audience. Do they ever doubt themselves in spite of their success? Did they ask their wives about how the novel's female characters should behave? Who did they think ought to play Stephen King if someone made a film about him? Owen King suggested Bill Hader from *Saturday Night Live*.

After the questions the event ended. Stephen and Owen King left the stage and the rest of us, hot and damp from sweat since there was no air condition in the church, headed for the exit to hand in our bracelets and in return receive a (hopefully signed) copy of the novel. Outside the church you heard occasional exclamations of joy when someone opened their book and found it signed. When I had stepped out and looked in mine, I was happy to find that my book had been signed by both Owen and Stephen King.

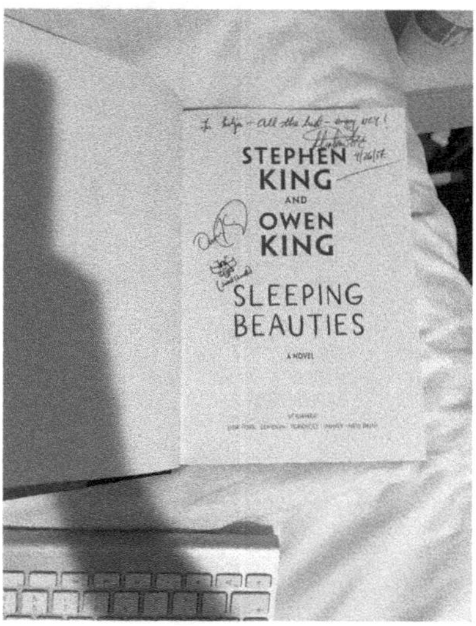

The next day it was time for me to head back to Sweden, and since I had spent only two days in New York I was still so jetlagged that I almost fell asleep at the airport before having boarded my plane. Finally on board I spent the hours crossing the Atlantic doing nothing else than eating and sleeping. Exhausted but happy.

## Holly: (not) a favorite

***"I'm fucked up, didn't you notice?"***

We first meet Holly Gibney, then in her late thirties, halfway into Stephen King's novel *Mr. Mercedes.* King has said that he initially intended her to be just a minor character in the story, but that he liked her so much that he gave her a much bigger part than he had originally visualized for her.

Exactly what is it that makes Holly so charming, aside from her being a movie buff who often refers to various films? In fact, initially not much, and that she would become one of King's favorite characters seems fairly unexpected. She is a subdued and shy woman with numerous diagnoses. She lives with her mother Charlotte in spite of getting close to 40. Charlotte totally controls her actions and opinions. In other words, she is no typical heroine. But all of those change during *Mr. Mercedes.*

The background story we are told about Holly is that she has been committed for psychiatric treatment twice, once in her teens and once during her twenties. Holly calls these two occasions her "total freakouts," to differentiate them from that "state of low to moderate freakout" in which she lived constantly.

Her first visit to the psychiatric ward was caused by Mike Sturdevant, when Holly was a high school sophomore hurrying from one classroom to the next in order to be noticed as little as possible. Already then, she was prone to anxiety attacks, depression, sleep problems, and, worst of all, she was stimming. Stimming is repetitive movements in order to balance feelings and sensory input.

Holly bit her nails and chewed her lips, but from around eight she had begun to hug herself, shiver throughout her body, mumble to herself and grimace. Those spells would last for five or ten seconds, after which she could carry on doing whatever she had been doing. She was hardly conscious of her behavior, except when her mother told her to stop shaking and making faces since people might think she was having a fit.

Mike Sturdevant lived on an entirely different level of the school's hierarchy than Holly, and normally wouldn't even have been aware of her existence, but one day he happened to catch sight of her when she was having one of her fits. Mike and his friends stopped and stared at her, and then Mike asked her what she was gibbering about.

"Gibbering!" Mike shouted. "Jibba-jibba-gibbering!" And from that moment on Holly was known as Jibba-Jibba at Walnut Hills High School, and so she remained until shortly after the Christmas recess, when her mother found her curled up naked in the bathroom, from which she stated that she never again wanted to enter Walnut Hills. If her mother tried to force her back, she would kill herself.

Her second incarceration was caused by her boss at the Frank Mitchell Fine Homes and Estates agency in Cincinnati. Frank Mitchell, Jr. claimed that her work was deficient, that her colleagues hated her and that the only way for her to keep her job was that he continued to have her back, which he would do if she slept with him. Holly was very close to succumb. She followed him into his office, where he began unbuttoning her blouse. After three buttons, she socked him in the face, his glasses flew off and his lip began bleeding. He called her various names and said that he would have her arrested for assault. Holly, on her part, threatened to report him for attempted rape, something he had also previously been accused of. Neither of them went to the police, but Holly solved the dilemma by coming to work very early one day and thrash Frank Mitchell, Jr.'s office. Later, she was found huddled in a corner of her own office, chewing her fingertips which were bleeding freely.

When Holly had gotten through her second total freakout she began working as an indexer for a small publishing company. Since the editor she met at her employment interview, Jim Haggerty, obviously knew nothing about indexing, Holly managed to relax and easily tell him how she would go about performing the work. Haggerty was impressed enough to hire her on the spot, but when times grew hard the small publisher went bankrupt. By then, Holly had already bought her first car and actually felt pretty well ... while she was working. Without work to do, she still felt penned up. She got a job at the local hospital and another one at the Cincinnati District Court where she handled claims.

When we first meet Holly in *Mr. Mercedes*, we do so via Janelle Patterson, Holly's cousin, who is in a relationship with Bill Hodges. Bill fairly quickly realises that Holly suffers from obsessive-compulsive disorder, synesthesia, some autism and in addition expresses herself entirely without filter. She often states facts without any regard for whether her statements may have negative consequences. King himself has described her as "an obsessive compulsive with a huge inferiority complex." But she also has an excellent memory, extremely keen observation skills, and is highly computer savvy.

There is no doubt that Holly's mother Charlotte has a strong hold on her, but gradually as her story unfolds in the Bill Hodges novels, she grows and becomes more self-sufficient. The first time Holly holds her own against her mother is while she, Bill and Bill's friend Jerome Robinson are searching the Mercedes killer Brady Hartsfield's cellar to find clues to what he is planning. Charlotte demands that Holly must come home, but Holly tells her that she is with her friends and intends to stay with them. This is the start of her emancipation.

Over the course of the novel, she grows stronger and stronger, though still fragile, and by the end she has moved away from her mother and, thanks to the inheritance of half a million dollars left her by Janelle, gotten her own apartment. She even offers to help Bill handle his computer work if he accepts the job as a bond agent offered to him.

When we meet her again in *Finders Keepers* and *End of Watch* she runs the detective bureau Finders Keepers together with Bill, handling the office and the computers while he is out in the field. She still has problems and still tells more than her listeners have asked for, but it is obvious that she has grown considerably during the four years since *Mr. Mercedes*. During the two new novels she keeps growing, and when Bill dies from pancreatic cancer at the end of *End of Watch* she takes over Finders Keepers, hires Pete Huntley, Bill's onetime partner who has now retired from his job with the police, as her new investigator, and is finally in full control of her work.

In *The Outsider* we meet Holly again. Here Alec Pelley, a retired policeman working for Terry Maitland's lawyer Howie Gold, employs her to try to figure out how Maitland could possibly have killed a young boy while evidently not being even in the same city. At the end of the novel, she joins forces with Ralph Anderson, a policeman in Flint City where the murder was committed, and they manage to solve the mystery. Holly is the same person we last met, but here she has a new partner to react to and act with, and this makes her grow further.

In Stephen King's novelette "If It Bleeds" she is finally given free rein and plays the lead part in the story. The story is set after the events in *The Outsider*, and Holly is again pitted against a similar being. She still runs Finders Keepers along with Pete Huntley, now on the fifth floor of the Drederics Building (the back door code is 4753, if you ever need it). They share the fifth floor with Furniture Imports, Inc., and David & Daughter, Forensic Accountants. Finders Keepers mainly gets work from law firms and insurance companies, while many private customers want them to find missing children and animals. Holly keeps to a firm pattern and every day at 3 P.M. sits down to watch her favorite TV show, the courtroom drama *John Law*. She always brings six Snickers bars – one for each commercial interruption.

Finally, in the eponymously titled novel *Holly*, we meet her for the fifth time, making her one of the fictional characters Stephen King has returned to most often. The year is now 2021 and we are back at the height of the Covid pandemic. Holly's mother has just died from the virus, having refused to take any vaccine against it. When informed about the estate by her mother's lawyer, Holly discovers that her mother Charlotte along with her brother, Holly's Uncle Henry (who is now in the grip of dementia), has stolen the money Holly inherited from Janey, and which they had told Holly was lost due to an unwise investment. Now the money resurfaces, and Holly is suddenly wealthy.

But we also notice that Holly is marked by what she has gone through. Earlier she loved horror movies, had seen every film about Jason, Michael, Freddy and the other monsters and could name every one of Christopher Lee's Dracula outings; lately she avoids horror movies, feeling that she has seen quite enough horror in reality. Another sign of the toll her experiences have taken is that she has begun smoking again, despite not wanting to and considering it unhealthy. But she just can't stay away.

We have learned much about Holly's mother, but all we know about her father is that he is long dead, was named Richard Gibney and worked as a traveling salesman for Ray Garton Farm Machinery, Inc., and consequently spent most of his time on the road, selling tractors and other utilities to farmers. When he was at home, Charlotte made certain that he knew exactly who made his household work.

The Holly stories have been filmed for TV. *Mr. Mercedes*, *Finders Keepers* and *End of Watch* were all mini-serials at AT&T's Audience Network, shown under the single series title *Mr. Mercedes* over the 2017–2019 seasons. In them, Holly was played by actress Justine Lupe (who has also read the English audiobook version of *Holly*) and who gave an excellent character interpretation. But when later HBO produced a miniseries of *The Outsider*, she wasn't given the chance of reprising her role. Now instead Cynthia Erivo played Holly, and apart from their very different appearances, Richard Price, *The Outsider*'s showrunner, decided to disregard everything that had happened to Holly in earlier stories, and to alter her personality as well: he toned her down drastically. In fact, Price chose neither to read any of the earlier novels nor to watch the serial based on them. You might find this a bit extreme, but Price even went so far as to ask Stephen King's permission to change Holly's name. This was where King put his foot down. He likes Holly, she would be in the story, and no arguments would sway him.

Will we hear more of Holly? Yes, indeed we will. In August 2023, Stephen King said that he was working on a novel titled *We Think Not*, and that Holly would be in it. Which feels logical, since after all she has decided to keep Finders Keepers going … and even has started watching horror films again.

## Stephen King in retirement?

***"I'm done. Done with writing books."***

In January 2002, Stephen King in a *Los Angeles Times* interview stated that he was going to retire. He wouldn't stop writing, but no further novels would be published, apart from those he was currently writing: a collection of stories called *Everything's Eventual*, a novel called *From a Buick 8*, and the three last "Dark Tower" novels. After that, it was enough.

"That's it. I'm done. Done writing books...You get to a point where you get to the edges of a room, and you can go back and go where you've been, and basically recycle stuff. I've seen it in my own work. People when they read *Buick Eight* are going think *Christine*. It's about a car that's not normal, OK? You say, 'I've said the things that I have to say, that are new and fresh and interesting to people.' Then you have a choice. You can either continue to go on, or say I left when I was still on top of my game. I left when I was still holding the ball, instead of it holding me."

His fans were naturally worried, and everyone who might know more about it was contacted and asked to give their views. Would King really retire? Even I had a phone call from a British radio show, *Meridian* on BBC World Service. I told them that I felt very doubtful about whether Stephen King really would stop publishing. Others who were asked included King's editor at Scribner, his American publisher, who said:

"The rumor is older than Methuselah, and yet he keeps writing and publishing. I've heard him describe a novel that I know he wants to write that isn't a part of *The Dark Tower* series, and that doesn't seem to duplicate anything he's done before. And since he's described it to me, it would be harsh and cruel for him to withhold it from me."

King's literary agent, Arthur Greene, also chimed in:

"He's spoken about retiring many times in the past. In my own mind, I think it's unlikely he'll stop working."

On Stephen King's web page, the whole thing was toned down:

"When asked on a recent episode of The View about his plans to retire, Stephen said that he has enough projects to keep him busy for the next 2 years and that he'll make a decision about retiring then. Don't worry, folks, finishing The Dark Tower books is first on the "to do list" during this next 2 years."

Finally, King himself felt forced to comment:

"When I said to that lady from the *LA Times* I might retire, I was still recovering from the accident that I was in. I was in a lot of pain, and I was under the pressure of finishing *The Dark Tower*. At that point, retirement looked good. When the pain went away and *The Dark Tower* finished up, retirement started to look bad."

And with that, the story ended. Since making that statement, Stephen King has published 37 books and has shown no signs of hanging up his typewriter – or nowadays, of course, computer. My guess is that retiring is something that may still sometimes feel alluring to him, but if so, is something he has chosen no longer to mention in public.

## Final retrospective thoughts

***And suddenly there was a new Stephen King book on display.***

Of course, you know the old saying, things were better back then. But were they really? Not if you like Stephen King and happen to live in Sweden, they weren't. Today, with the Internet and the ease with which you can communicate with others around the globe, life is actually much easier for those of us who like King and want to read everything he publishes as soon as possible.

Nonetheless, much has happened during the fifty years since King published his first book. Today we take many things for granted we certainly didn't back then, before the Internet and all other technical innovations over the last half century. If you like a particular musical entertainer or group, chances were fairly good that at some point they might pass near you on some tour. But authors never did, nor do they today. And truth to tell, when it comes to authors their fans are in most cases more interested in their writing than in their personalities, as opposed to fans of actors or performers who often display a totally different kind of personal idolatry.

But in King's case, his fans are primarily interested in his stories. This was true also for me during the 1980s and 1990s, when you had no idea of whether a new novel or film was in the making. Today we know about those things long before we have the chance of enjoying them. We know when King is working on a novel, and we know something of what it will be about; months in advance we know its title and exactly when it will be released. In the 1980s, you walked into a bookstore and suddenly there was a new Stephen King book on display. Probably a book which has already been on sale for a year or two before being translated into Swedish. Swedish publishers were not known for their speed in translating his books. On that account, the almost bizarre record is held by *The Dark Tower 3: The Waste Lands*, which had to wait for sixteen years before being translated into Swedish.

In all honesty, though I won't deny that it also was a quite wonderful feeling to find that unheard-of and brand new Stephen King novel in a bookstore, to immediately buy it (if you happened to be able to afford it), to get back home and start reading it. I can miss that feeling nowadays. Certainly, it is always a special thing to open a new book by King, but that other feeling of surprise and unexpected joy is no longer there.

Getting hold of books in English was even harder, and if you also were insufficiently versed in the language, it simply was no alternative. Indeed, one of my most embarrassing memories connected to Stephen King has to do with knowledge of the English language, or perhaps more precisely with the lack of such knowledge. For quite a while I believed that the second "Dark Tower" book, *The Drawing of the Three*, was actually a book about King writing the third book in the series: in my mind, I translated the title to "The Writing of the Third." Trust me when I say that it felt truly awkward to admit my mistake even to myself. And besides, of course, I have also learned that "drawing" means making pictures, not writing texts. Oh well.

During the later half of the 1990s, Internet began its triumphal march, and everything became easier, even though most of us had no idea of how to create a web page. Most of them were just huge amounts of text, which was fine in itself, but there were also large numbers of revolving skulls which everyone imagined looked cool, and a few pictures which you usually were unable to see since it took too long for them to load if all you had was a 28 or 56 bps modem. But if you could bear to disregard this, the world suddenly opened in front of you. People in the US told you when new books were about to be published. You had an opportunity to improve your English. You got to know people with the same interests as you, all around the world.

It was then – in 1996 – I started ”Lilja's Library – The World of Stephen King.” And yes, I, too, had some revolving skulls, red text on black, and a lot of other things nobody today would even think of putting on their web pages. My main reason for starting the page was that no web page collecting all the information I myself wanted about Stephen King and his work existed. There were some King-related pages to be found, but mostly they focused on some particular aspect or part of his writing. Certainly, there were quite a few communities where King and his work was discussed, but what I felt was missing from the net was a single place where all information available was collected, and that was what I tried to create: a place where anyone could find everything about Stephen King's work.

Gradually, as the net grew, it became continuously more easy to find the books you were looking for, but booksellers in my part of the world still resisted importing English books. Back then, they certainly didn't import British or American books and keep them on their shelves, as some of them now do you had to special order them, and that was definitively not cheap.

Add to this that gradually also audiobooks began to become huge in Sweden, so that companies like Storytel and Bookbeat now offer entire libraries. This, in conjunction with web stores and ebooks (yes, I am aware that some people don't consider ebooks to be ”real” books, but even so ...), has made life much easier when it comes to quickly getting hold of books at a reasonable price.

Then there used to be a problem with all those short stories published in magazines, mainly in the US. You had no idea even of their existence, and when you found out about them, there was still no way of getting hold of them. This problem too was solved by the Internet. Thanks to the net, the era of collectors sending stories back and forth among themselves began. If you had missed out on some particular story, there was always someone who had it, and after a while you yourself usually had something to trade it for. Photostat machines ran hot, and stamps were bought. And don't forget that this was before you were able to email large attachments to each other.

The Internet also brought the chance of starting to hunt for books published in limited editions. I well remember buying a copy of Stephen King's *Six Stories*. This was after I had started "Lilja's Library" and had made a few friends in the US, who kept me updated on what was happening. I decided to go for it and buy my first limited edition Stephen King book. *Six Stories* was a small paperback story collection published by King's own Philtrum Press in 1997, in an edition of 1,100 numbered and signed copies. The publisher's price for the book was $80. Today, I'm very happy to have bought it. It still holds its place in my bookshelf.

I already mentioned audiobooks. That market as well has lately exploded. Though far from all of Stephen King's books are available as audiobooks in Sweden, it is happily easy to get them in English language editions. In many cases King himself has read his work, so all you need to do is put your earphones on and press play – which was unthinkable as late as the 1990s. Back then, a handful of titles were available for those of us who couldn't prove that our eyesight was so bad that we were allowed to borrow from the audiobooks produced exclusively for libraries to lend to persons hard of seeing. And the problem with those particular books is that they are so ineptly produced that it is unbearable to listen to them. Whoever makes them seem to think that if people can't see, they also have no imagination and consequently no need for any passion or empathy in those who read books for them. The readers of these books keep their voices absolutely level throughout entire novels. They neither raise nor lower it, nor sound more or less excited when things happen. At best, you feel that they are reading an exceptionally dull grocery list. They also pause in the middle of sentences, not just between them as normal persons. These "books for blind" are genuinely awful, and I can think of nobody who deserves the fate of having to read books in such a fashion. Which of course never stopped me from borrowing all of King's available spoken word books and copy them to cassettes of my own to listen from. You know what they say. You make do with what's available.

On the whole, then, we must conclude that at least from the perspective of a Stephen King fan, existence has improved over these last fifty years, and most particularly it has become easier. What will happen in the future remains to be seen, for even if Stephen King decides not to keep writing for another fifty years, I feel reasonably confident that it will be a long time before we see him tell his last story.

# Afterword

Stephen King has published books for all of fifty years. Some of you have followed him for all of that time, others for only a few years. Personally, I've been along for 41 of those years. But regardless of how long, we have all read Stephen King. We have all experienced the feeling of opening a brand new Stephen King book for the first time.

But have you ever reflected on how lucky we are, who of all the 4,5 billion years the Earth has existed have managed to be born at just the right time to be here at the same time as Stephen King? A hundred years earlier, or a hundred years later, and we would have missed it. Never forget that.

Thanks for taking the time to read my little book!

Hans-Åke Lilja
Örebro, January 26, 2024

# Author's note

Before we part ways, I would like to thank a number of people who have helped make this book what it is.

Anders Jakobson is my comrade-in-arms when it comes to Stephen King. Together, we have travelled to both London and Hamburg to meet King. Besides having given much valuable feedback on this book, he wrote a large part of the subchapter entitled ”Four days in London in 2006” when it was originally published on our website ”Följeslagarna,” as well as the interview with Peter Straub in the subchapter ”Working with a King: Peter Straub,” and the Swedish translation of it.

My other manuscript readers – Louise Laver, Christian Sjöblom and Carina Holm: thank you for excellent input.

My Swedish publisher, Ekström & Garay, for continuing to believe in me and for publishing this book.

Stephen King, who again is the source of everything discussed in the book.

My thanks to you all!

# Index 1: Books by Stephen King

Titles and year of appearance reflect the U.S. editions of the books.

**The first decade**

1. Carrie (April 4, 1974)
2. 'Salem's Lot (October 17, 1975)
3. The Shining (January 28, 1977)
4. Rage. Under the name Richard Bachman (September 13, 1977)
5. Night Shift (February 1978)
6. The Stand (September 1978)
7. The Long Walk. Under the name Richard Bachman (July 1979)
8. The Dead Zone (August 30, 1979)
9. Firestarter (September 29, 1980)
10. Danse Macabre (April 20, 1981)
11. Roadwork. Under the name Richard Bachman (March 1981)
12. Cujo (September 8, 1981)
13. The Running Man. Under the name Richard Bachman (May 1982)
14. The Dark Tower I – The Gunslinger (June 10, 1982)
15. Different Seasons (August 27, 1982)
16. Christine (April 29, 1983)
17. Cycle of The Werewolf (November 1983)
18. Pet Sematary (November 17, 1983)

**The second decade**

19. The Talisman. With Peter Straub (November 8, 1984)
20. Thinner. Under the name Richard Bachman (November 19, 1984)
21. The Eyes of The Dragon (December 10, 1984 [limited])
22. Skeleton Crew (June 21, 1985)

23. It (September 15, 1986)
24. The Dark Tower II – The Drawing Of The Three (May 1987)
25. Misery (June 8, 1987)
26. The Tommyknockers (November 10, 1987)
27. Nightmares in the Sky (November 1988)
28. The Dark Half (October 20, 1989)
29. The Stand – The Complete And Uncut Edition (May 1990)
30. Four Past Midnight (September 1990)
31. The Dark Tower III – The Waste Lands (August 1991)
32. Needful Things (October 1991)
33. Gerald's Game (May 1992)
34. Dolores Claiborne (November 1992)
35. Nightmares and Dreamscapes (September 29, 1993)

**The third decade**

36. Insomnia (September 18, 1994)
37. Rose Madder (June 1995)
38.1. The Green Mile 1 – The Two Dead Girls (March 28, 1996)
38.2. The Green Mile 2 – The Mouse on the Mile (April 25, 1996)
38.3. The Green Mile 3 – Coffey's Hands (May 30, 1996)
38.4. The Green Mile 4 – The Bad Death of Eduardo Delacroix (June 27, 1996)
38.5. The Green Mile 5 – Night Journey (July 25, 1996)
38.6. The Green Mile 6 – Coffey on the Mile (August 29, 1996)
39. Desperation (September 24, 1996)
40. The Regulators. Under the name Richard Bachman (September 24, 1996)
41. The Dark Tower IV – Wizard and Glass (November 4, 1997)
42. Bag of Bones (September 22, 1998)
43. Storm of the Century (February 1, 1999)
44. The Girl Who Loved Tom Gordon (April 6, 1999)
45. Hearts in Atlantis (September 14, 1999)
46. Secret Windows (October 2000)

47. On Writing: A Memoir of the Craft (October 3, 2000)
48. Dreamcatcher (March 20, 2001)
49. Black House. With Peter Straub (September 15, 2001)
50. Everything's Eventual (March 19, 2002)
51. From a Buick 8 (September 24, 2002)
52. The Dark Tower I – The Gunslinger (revised and expanded edition) (June 23, 2003)
53. The Dark Tower V – Wolves of the Calla (November 4, 2003)

**The fourth decade**

54. The Dark Tower VI – Song of Susannah (June 8, 2004)
55. The Dark Tower VII – The Dark Tower (September 21, 2004)
56. Faithful: Two Diehard Boston Red Sox Fans Chronicle the 2004 Season. With Stewart O'Nan (December 2, 2004)
57. The Colorado Kid (Original paperback edition) (October 4, 2005)
58. Cell (January 24, 2006)
59. Lisey's Story (October 24, 2006)
60. Blaze. Under the name Richard Bachman (June 12, 2007)
61. Duma Key (January 22, 2008)
62. Just After Sunset (November 11, 2008)
63. Under the Dome (November 10, 2009)
64. Blockade Billy (April 20, 2010)
65. Full Dark, No Stars (November 9, 2010)
66. 11/22/63 (November 8, 2011)
67. The Wind Through the Keyhole (February 21, 2012)
68. Ghost Brothers of Darkland County (June 4, 2013)
69. Joyland (June 4, 2013)
70. Doctor Sleep (September 24, 2013)

**The fifth decade**

71. Mr Mercedes (June 3, 2014)
72. Revival (November 11, 2014)

73. Finders Keepers (June 2, 2015)
74. The Bazaar of Bad Dreams (November 3, 2015)
75. End of Watch (July 7, 2016)
76. Hearts in Suspension (November 7, 2016)
77. Charlie the Choo-Choo (November 22, 2016)
78. Gwendy's Button Box. With Richard Chizmar (May 16, 2017)
79. Sleeping Beauties. With Owen King (September 26, 2017)
80. The Outsider (May 22, 2018)
81. Elevation (October 30, 2018)
82. The Institute (September 10, 2019)
83. If It Bleeds (May 5, 2020)
84. Later (March 2, 2021)
85. Billy Summers (August 3, 2021)
86. Gwendy's Final Task. With Richard Chizmar (February 15, 2022)
87. Fairy Tale (September 6, 2022)
88. Holly (September 5, 2023)

# Index 2: Novels and short stories set in part or entirely in Castle Rock

The Body (Different Seasons, 1982)

Cujo (1981)

The Dark Half (1989)

Dead Zone (1979)

Drunken Fireworks (The Bazaar of Bad Dreams, 2015)

Elevation (2018)

Gramma (Skeleton Crew, 1985)

Gwendy's Button Box (2017)

Gwendy's Final Task (2022)

It Grows on You (Nightmares & Dreamscapes, 1993)

Mrs Todd's Shortcut (Skeleton Crew, 1985)

Needful Things (1991)

Nona (Skeleton Crew, 1985)

Premium Harmony (The Bazaar of Bad Dreams, 2015)

Sundog (Four Past Midnight, 1990)

Uncle Otto's Truck (Skeleton Crew, 1985)

# Index 3: Novels and short stories mentioning Castle Rock

11/22/63 (2011)

A Good Marriage (Full Dark, No Stars, 2010)

Bag of Bones (1998)

Blaze (2007)

The Dark Half (1989)

The Dark Tower 7 (2004)

Doctor Sleep (2013)

Dreamcatcher (2001)

Eyes of the Dragon (1984)

Gerald's Game (1992)

The Girl Who Loved Tom Gordon (1999)

Gwendy's Button Box (2017)

Gwendy's Final Task (2022)

IT (1986)

Lisey's Stories (2006)

The Man in the Black Suit (Everything's Eventual, 2002)

Mr Harrigan's telephone (If it Bleeds, 2020)

N. (Just After Sunset, 2008)

Pet Sematary (1983)

Revival (2014)

Riding the Bullet (Everything's Eventual, 2002)

Rita Hayworth and The Shawshank Redemption (Different Seasons, 1982)

The Stand - Uncut (1990)

Under the Dome (2009)

# Index 4: Novels and short stories by other authors mentioning Castle Rock

Gwendy's Magic Feather (2019)
By Richard Chizmar

One on one (1993)
By Tabitha King

# Index 5: Novels and short stories set in part or entirely in Derry

11/22/63 (2011)

Bag of Bones (1998)

The Bird and the Album (A Fantasy Reader, 1981)

Dreamcatcher (2001)

Fair Extension (Full Dark, No Stars, 2010)

Insomnia (1994)

IT (1986)

The Road Virus Head North (Everything's Eventual, 2002)

Secret Window, Secret Garden (Four Past Midnight, 1990)

# Index 6: Novels and short stories mentioning Derry

Autopsy Room 4 (Everything's Eventual, 2002)

The Body (Different Seasons, 1982)

The Dark Tower 7 (2004)

Gerald's Game (1992)

Gwendy's Final Task (2022)

Hearts in Atlantis (1999)

Lisey's Story (2006)

Misery (1987)

Mrs Todd's Shortcut (Skeleton Crew, 1985)

Mute (Just After Sunset, 2008)

Needful Things (1991)

The Night Flier (Nightmares & Dreamscapes, 1993)

On Slide Inn Road (Esquire, 2020)

Pet Sematary (1983)

The Running Man (1982)

Storm of the Century (1999)

The Tommyknockers (1987)

Uncle Otto's Truck (Skeleton Crew, 1985)

Under The Dome (2009)

# Index 7: Novels and short stories by other authors mentioning Derry

Gwendy's Magic Feather (2019)
By Richard Chizmar

Horns (2010)
By Joe Hill

NOS4A2 (2013)
By Joe Hill

One on one (1993)
By Tabitha King

# Index 8: Movies based on books by Stephen King

Titles and year of appearance reflect the U.S. premier.

**The first decade**

1. Carrie (1976)
2. The Shining (1980)
3. Creepshow (1982)
4. Cujo (1983)
5. The Dead Zone (1983)
6. Christine (1983)

**The second decade**

7. Children Of The Corn (1984)
8. Firestarter (1984)
9. Cat's Eye (1985)
10. Silver Bullet (1985)
11. Stephen King's (1985)
12. Maximum Overdrive (1986)
13. Stand By Me (1986)
14. Creepshow 2 (1987)
15. The Running Man (1987)
16. Pet Sematary (1989)
17. The Cat From Hell (1990)
18. Graveyard Shift (1990)
19. Misery (1990)
20. The Lawnmower Man (1992)
21. Sleepwalkers (1992)
22. The Dark Half (1993)
23. Needful Things (1993)

**The third decade**

24. The Shawshank Redemption (1994)
25. The Mangler (1995)
26. Dolores Claiborne (1995)
27. Stephen King's Nightshift Collection (1995)
28. Thinner (1996)
29. Apt Pupil (1998)
30. The Green Mile (1999)
31. Hearts in Atlantis (2001)
32. Dreamcatcher (2003)

**The fourth decade**

33. Secret Window (2004)
34. Riding the Bullet (2004)
35. 1408 (2007)
36. The Mist (2007)
37. Dolan's Cadillac (2009)
38. Carrie (2013)

**The fifth decade**

39. A Good Marriage (2014)
40. Big Driver (2014)
41. Mercy (2014)
42. Cell (2016)
43. The Dark Tower (2017)
44. IT: part 1 (2017)
45. Pet Sematary (2019)
46. IT: part 2 (2019)
47. Doctor Sleep (2019)
48. Firestarter (2022)
49. The Boogeyman (2023)

# Index 9:TV series and TVmovies based on books by Stephen King

Titles and year of appearance reflect the U.S. airdate.

**The first decade**

1. 'Salem's Lot (1979)

**The second decade**

2. Word Processor Of The Gods (1985)
3. Gramma (1986)
4. Sorry, Right Number (1987)
5. It (1990)
6. Sometimes They Come Back (1991)
7. Golden Years (1991)
8. The Moving Finger (1992)
9. The Tommyknockers (1993)

**The third decade**

10. The Stand (1994)
11. The Langoliers (1995)
12. The Shining (1997)
13. Chattery Teeth (1997)
14. Revelations Of Becka Paulson (1997)
15. Trucks (1997)
16. The Night Flier (1997)
17. Chinga (1998)
18. Storm Of The Century (1999)
19. Rose Red (2002)
20. The Dead Zone (2002-2007)

21. Stephen King's Kingdom Hospital (2004)

**The fourth decade**

22. 'Salem's Lot [A two part miniseries] (2004)
23. Desperation (2006)
24. Nightmares & Dreamscapes (2006)
25. Children of the Corn (2009)
26. Haven (2010-2014)
27. Bag of Bones (2011)
28. Under the Dome (2013-2015)

**The fifth decade**

29. 11.22.63 (2016)
30. The Mist (2017)
31. Mr Mercedes (2017-2019)
32. Gerald's Game (2017)
33. 1922 (2017)
34. Castle Rock (2018-2019)
35. In the Tall Grass (2019)
36. The Outsider (2020)
37. The Stand (2020)
38. Lisey's Story (2021)
39. Chapelwaite (2021)
40. Mr Harrigan's Phone (2022)

## Index 10: Sequels based on books by Stephen King

Titles and year of appearance reflect the U.S. premier.

**The second decade**

1. A Return To 'Salem's Lot (1987)
2. Pet Sematary 2 (1992)
3. Children Of The Corn 2 – The Final Sacrifice (1992)

**The third decade**

4. Children Of The Corn 3 – Urban Harvest (1995)
5. The Lawnmower Man 2 – Beyond Cyberspace (1995)
6. Sometimes They Come Back ... Again (1996)
7. Children Of The Corn 4 – The Gathering (1996)
8. Children of the Corn 5: Fields of Terror (1998)
9. Sometimes They Come Back ... For More (1999)
10. The Rage: Carrie 2 (1999)
11. Children Of The Corn 666: Isaac's Return (1999)
12. Children of the Corn: Revelation (2001)
13. The Mangler 2 (2002)
14. Firestarter: Rekindled (2002)

**The fourth decade**

15. The Mangler Reborn (2005)
16. Children of the Corn: Genesis (2011)

**The fifth decade**

17. Children of the Corn: Runaway (2018)
18. Children of the Corn (2023)
19. Pet Sematary: Bloodlines (2023)

Milton Keynes UK
Ingram Content Group UK Ltd.
UKHW022209221024
449899UK00006B/47

9 798887 715735